G.O.R.E SECTOR
BOOK 6

RAMPAGE

A NOVEL BY MICHAEL COLE

SEVEREDPRESS

RAMPAGE

Copyright © 2025 by MICHAEL COLE

WWW.SEVEREDPRESS.COM

ISBN: 978-1-923663-03-9

CHAPTER 1

"I'm telling you, this is a monumental mistake."

Senator Stephen Yuel was more than used to General Austin Kilmore's shrill tone. To the men and women in G.O.R.E. Sector, he rarely raised his voice. He never had to; he had the respect of each and every one of them. All he had to do was state an order and it was followed, and if there was a problem, it was brought to his attention and dealt with. But the senator did not fall under his command. Like many politicians, he had been in so-called 'service' far too long and now saw himself as a higher class of human.

Senator Yuel was a man in his mid-sixties. He was a head shorter than the general, walked with a cane, and had glasses with thick brown rims.

Behind him was the Granger Valley Research Complex. A large steel structure in the middle of nowhere, it was set to be the new home for the X41 particle sample retrieved by Raptor Pack on the island of Zil Nesans, located in the archipelago of Lasenn Baryer.

For two months, X41 and the liquified samples from the secret laboratory were securely stored in a G.O.R.E. Sector holding facility in Texas, with only a select handful of personnel granted access to it. It was there, and only there, where General Kilmore felt comfortable keeping the samples, with plenty of manpower and firepower stationed all around it.

Since the acquiring of the samples, plenty of governmental figures tried to place their hands in the pot, each with their own ideas of how to utilize the findings. Much to Kilmore's discomfort, but not to his surprise, many of them wanted the samples experimented on for weapons research.

For two months, he made his case. This was a substance that could not be controlled, citing Brom-Caylen's twice failed experiments and the disasters that followed. It was an argument that worked against him, since it technically was not 'proven' in an official capacity that Brom-Caylen was involved in any research regarding the particle.

Government officials, while claiming they worked for the general public, often paid more attention to various figures they had quid pro quo deals with. 'Scratch my back, I'll fund your reelection campaign, not to mention give you a cut of the profits.' Needless to say, arms dealers were eager to get their hands on the samples, and only through the politicians could they pry them from G.O.R.E. Sector.

Sadly, the effort eventually grew successful. Senator Yuel, the majority leader, successfully got into President Chris Hudson's ear and convinced him to relocate X41 to the old nuclear facility in Granger Valley, and for a few hand-picked physicists to have access.

Senator Yuel went a step further. While it was allowed for G.O.R.E. Sector to provide security assistance to the site, the primary security forces would be from a group called Trident.

Kilmore was no fool. He knew precisely why Yuel went with that specific company. For one, they belonged to a weapons manufacturer whom he and many other government officials were partnered with. Two, he did not want too many G.O.R.E. Sector employees on site, for he wanted to limit Kilmore's influence as much as possible.

"The mistake is yours," the senator replied to Kilmore. "What we have is invaluable, and you'd rather let it rot in a bunker, deep underground. We have a golden opportunity to create something incredible. Maybe even find a way to use the particles against any mutation that may arise in the future."

Kilmore closed his eyes and clenched his jaw. He heard the words, but more importantly, sensed the real meaning. When Yuel said 'mutation' he meant 'enemy', and by that, he was referring to nations and groups. Politicians were always eager for war, even though most of them had no skin in the game.

When he opened his eyes, he watched a few men in grey tactical uniforms patrolling around the center complex. Just by the looks on their faces, these guys had no idea what they were getting involved in. To them, it was just another job. In the holding facility in Texas, every G.O.R.E. Sector individual, whether they were deep in the facility or working outside at the gates, was constantly on edge. They understood the subject in the storage facility could produce monstrosities unlike anything the world had ever seen.

But the guys here saw it as nothing more than a rock. To Yuel, that did not matter. He just wanted them to be loyal to his cause.

"Tomorrow's the big day," the senator continued. "I expect the package here at ten-hundred. Don't forget the liquified samples as well."

Kilmore dabbed his forehead. The Arizona heat was not to his liking, especially when he was already heating up with anger from the sound of Yuel's voice.

"I know where you can stick them," he remarked.

He turned around and walked away to the MEAV M1 in which he traveled in. Two G.O.R.E. Sector pilots waited at its ramp, ready to take him into the sky. Like the general, they were visibly displeased with the senator's interference.

"Funny," the lead pilot quipped to Kilmore. "They're all about 'listen to the experts' unless the experts are *us*."

"Ain't that the truth?" Kilmore replied. He returned the pilots' salute and took a seat. "Let's get moving, gentlemen. We're a courier service today." He strapped himself in and looked out the window. "Captain Rodney and the others aren't going to be pleased."

CHAPTER 2

"Rotate turret twelve degrees… Target ascending to thirty meters…"

Thomas Rodney watched the drone through the lens of his long-range binoculars. Its sides were painted yellow and black in a comical effort to mimic the appearance of a giant bee.

On the ground in the middle of the valley was one of Howard Tate's latest inventions. Mountain Lions, as he called them, were quadrupedal robots, roughly eleven feet in length, equipped with a twenty-millimeter turret on their backs as well as short-range plasma guns in their 'mouths'. From afar, the thing did resemble a large cat, though one with silver armor and a big gun protruding from between its shoulder blades.

Its rear legs bent, allowing it to aim the turret skyward. Its barrel rotated to the right, following the captain's commands.

"Fire when ready."

Howard deliberately zigzagged the drone, testing the mechanical soldier's ability to track the target.

The mountain lion traced its movements, calculated its trajectory, and unloaded a burst of ammunition.

Like a balloon made of carbon fiber, the drone burst in midair.

The mountain lion leveled out and moved over to inspect the remains and confirm the 'kill'.

Charity stepped alongside Thomas and presented the handheld monitor, displaying the unit's point of view on the screen. Digital crosshairs passed over the drone's remains, flashing green after declaring the target neutralized.

"I guess we'll have to stop making fun of Howard," she said. "At least, in regard to his claims of making his own *Battle Cat.*"

"Glad you made that clarification," Renee said. "Because we'll never run out of reasons to stop making fun of Howard."

The engineer approached from the other side of their observation tent, holding the now-useless control board for the drone.

"Lovely. Good to have friends."

"Ah, you're just mad because we made you sacrifice one of your precious robots as target practice," Charity said.

Howard shrugged, confirming some truth to that statement.

"Now that we know the weapons system works, I say it's time to see how they do in close quarters," Thomas said. He put his microphone to his lips. "Come on back."

Like a good dog, the machine turned around and started galloping towards Raptor Pack's location.

A proximity alert chimed from within *Firebird Two*. Archer, seated near the bow—with his sniper rifle in hand, of course—entered the cockpit to get a glance at the radar. He reappeared a moment later and gave the team a half nod, confirming the source of the signal.

General Kilmore was on approach. Given the fact he was coming straight for their location, he was probably coming with bad news.

"I'm assuming the meeting to appeal the government's decision went poorly," Renee said.

"We'll know in a minute," Thomas said. He did not bother hiding the frustration in his voice. Like Kilmore, he had his suspicions about the motivations of the senators and congressmen who wanted the X41 sample moved. Ever since they defeated Moran's crew and collected the sample from Zil Nesans, they had been fighting a new battle. It was one of words and influence, and unlike most of G.O.R.E. Sector's wars, they could not shoot their way to victory.

There was no doubt in Thomas' mind that Brom-Caylen had their hands in the pockets of many powerful people. The current U.S. president, Chris Hudson, while well-meaning, had a tendency to lean heavily on the so-called wisdom of other career politicians. Though he often deferred to General Kilmore's wisdom, there were just too many influential voices calling for increased research into the meteorite sample.

The MEAV appeared on the horizon. Not too long ago, it was a machine that inspired awe from the members of Raptor Pack. It closely resembled *Firebird-One* and was equipped with the same armaments.

Two months ago, Renee would have pouted at the idea of someone else piloting a MEAV M1. Now, she had to resist laughing like a middle-school kid on the playground, for she had the MEAV M2.

Firebird-Two was a vast improvement over the original design. It was twice the size of the original model and was designed with reconnaissance missions in mind. Its inside consisted of a small, but proper laboratory for Howard and Charity to perform their analysis. Despite its size, the machine was just as fast and maneuverable as the first one, thanks to increased engine power. Howard's new ion fuel cell would likely score him a billion dollars and global demand had he not signed an exclusive deal with G.O.R.E. Sector. At the very least, it earned him tenure and a very generous retirement package.

It came complete with cots for sleeping, desks for the two scientists, and one for Thomas. The inside of the aircraft was a real life workstation, complete with a boatload of weapons and ammo.

Even Archer had his stations. On the port and starboard sides were turret control systems where he could manually operate a fifty-caliber machine gun turret with a secondary incendiary barrel. It was a control system straight out of *Star Wars*, except he would not be firing at *tie fighters*, but violent monsters. And given the encounter with Moran two months back, possibly enemy helicopters.

Within a minute, the MEAV M1 was overhead. It lowered to the dusty testing grounds, the ion thrusters kicking up tan clouds.

The aft ramp lowered. Stepping down its slope was an agitated looking General Kilmore.

"Yep. Bad news," Renee said.

"Is it that obvious?" the general quipped. He stood by the small tent Thomas had set up to observe the testing and gazed at the mountain lion. "How's Dr. Tate's new toys?"

The engineer leaned back as though physically hit by the question. "Can't believe you have to ask."

Thomas laughed. "They're doing pretty well so far." He directed Kilmore's attention to a set of concrete barricades to their ten o'clock. They were fifty yards out and stood twelve feet high. "We are just now testing its close quarters capabilities."

He looked to Charity. She manually operated the machine with her tablet. The mountain lion turned clockwise, pointing its cockpit-shaped head to the concrete barricades. From its eyes came an invisible laser, which connected with the three targets.

On the screen, three red crosshairs appeared.

"No projectiles," Thomas said into the microphone. "Engage targets and exterminate."

The mountain lion galloped over to the concrete walls. It closed in on the middle one, leaned onto its back legs, and rammed its front arms into the bricks. The barricade burst into numerous pieces, the metal limbs suffering nothing more than minor scratches.

It twisted to the right and swung its arm in a clawing motion, taking off the top of the next barricade. A second swipe broke the thing in half at its center.

The third target was knocked down in one large piece as the robot leapt on it like a lion tackling an antelope. Pinning the 'enemy' to the ground, it proceeded to bash it until no trace of its original form remained.

"Hmm. Not bad," Kilmore said, watching the demonstration through his own set of binoculars.

The machine turned to face him. From across the field, a mechanical voice boomed.

"Piece of cake, Captain."

Thomas stared at it for a moment, then looked over at Howard, who was leaning close to a microphone.

"Really? You added a loudspeaker to the thing?"

"Of course!" Howard exclaimed. "Firstly, it helps to have the machine be able to verbally communicate with personnel on the field. Secondly, it's fun to trash-talk enemies."

"Our enemies are *monsters*," Charity said.

Howard waved dismissively. "Eh, you're just jealous that I'm the one who constructed such a perfect robot."

"Mmm." Thomas lowered his glasses. "Not sure perfect's the word. Took about fifteen seconds to destroy the targets. Should've pulled it off in eight."

Howard scowled. "Uh-huh!"

"I could've handled it in one-point-five," Archer chimed in, tilting his rifle muzzle up.

Howard snorted. True to form, the team could not let him enjoy the glory of the moment.

"I tried to sell the general on the idea of cloning a hundred other Ray Archers, but got overruled. Since we can't have you in a hundred different places at once, and would like to minimize casualties, the machines are next in line." He pointed his thumb at the wreck barricades. "Oh, and sometimes, we can't use firearms and artillery on a target. If a friendly is close by, maybe pinned down, we need a way of physically engaging the threat."

"It's nice that we don't have to manually control them," Thomas added. "Just lase the target and give a verbal command, and the computer knows what to do."

Howard perked up. "Look at that. Cap's saying something nice about my work, for once."

Thomas smiled. Of course, he saw the engineer's work as invaluable, and Howard knew this. But, Thomas could not just say that. After all, it was more fun to bust the guy's chops.

"Though, I had to repeat myself once or twice."

Howard slapped his pantlegs and leaned his head back. "Maybe if you didn't speak as though you had a mouthful of steak."

The captain raised his eyebrows and nodded at the appetizing thought. "We *are* in Texas."

"Before we have that steak, we've got another trip to make," General Kilmore said.

The team gave him their undivided attention, dreading the obvious bad news.

"X41's still going to Granger, huh?" Renee said.

Kilmore nodded. "I'm afraid so."

Thomas broke away from the group, hands on his hips, shaking his head. "Those dumb idiots. All they're going to do is cause more trouble. And we'll be the ones cleaning up their mess."

"That's what I told them," Kilmore replied. "Even after everything the world has seen, after every bloodthirsty bastardization of nature that has emerged since the meteor storm, after the crisis in Ramsey County that could have had world-wide repercussions, they still don't listen to me."

Renee, sharing his irritation, crushed her coffee cup in her fist.

"Do they seriously think they can control the particle? What exactly do they plan on doing with it? It's not like you can make bullets out of it. Anything it touches it corrupts."

"My theory is they do, in fact, believe they can control certain mutations," Kilmore said. "Of course, that's not what they say."

Thomas scoffed. "Sure. What they're probably saying is they can develop a cure. As though we haven't been attempting to figure that out."

"They think they can do it better," Charity said.

"More importantly, they don't care that much," Kilmore added. "I think they want to develop what I call 'controlled mutation'."

Howard winced at the implication. "Like… super soldiers?"

Kilmore shrugged. "It's anyone's guess. Personally, I think that's on the table. Secondly, I think they want to use animals, like dogs, to be used in warfare. Plus, there's probably the hope they can develop some sort of chemical weapon from the particle."

"I'll give you the short version," Thomas said. "Hubris. All they're going to do is create more hazards that *we* will have to fix. Worse, some of the samples will go 'missing' and wind up in the hands of some foreign government or terrorist group. Whoever pays the most."

He took a breath and looked at the rocket pods on *Firebird-Two*.

"Maybe we should just blow up the meteorite and the serum vials."

General Kilmore sighed. "Back on that island, I was thinking a similar thing. I gave half a thought to loading up all of the samples and disposing of them. Drop them into hot lead, shoot them into space...hell, drop them into one of those underground nuclear testing pits. But I convinced myself that some good may come from it; that Charity or somebody would be able to devise a method to maybe reverse the mutation or develop something to make all life on earth immune to the particles. A bit of a longshot, I know, but I guess I'm feeling hopeful in my old age."

He stepped away from the group and looked into the distance. It was a little after seven PM. The sun was still high in the sky, though gradually sinking into the west, signaling the end of their day and the beginning of someone else's.

"You okay there, General?" Renee asked.

Kilmore tucked his hands behind his back, watching the beautiful valley. There were a few small critters moving in the distance, emerging from hiding after scattering from the thunderous sounds of machine gun fire. There were some ferns growing to the east. Above them, a large moth had emerged and took to the sky, having gotten sufficient rest in the natural shade.

After a few moments, it became clear to Raptor Pack what was on the general's mind.

Peace. It was something the general did not get to experience too often. Even if they weren't in the middle of a fight, their time was spent preparing for the next one. And the next one. And the next. And the next. On, and on, and on.

They had gotten used to it, and for good reason; it was true.

Having grown so accustomed to their lives, none of Raptor Pack had given much thought to the endgame. Was this their destiny; fighting monsters until the end of time?

"You know, I'd like to see the sun rise on a world free of monsters," Kilmore said. "I guess I'm only now coming to terms with the fact that I won't live long enough to see such a morning. I'm in good shape and I plan on being here for a good while longer. And if anyone mentions retirement, I'll feed you to one of those things out there. But I have to face the facts: there's no stopping this thing anytime soon."

He turned around and looked at the five team members. In this moment, he did not look like a general, but a father admiring his kids.

"I need you all to promise me something? I want you to experience what I know I will not—rid the world of mutations. Permanently. And experience a sunset like this one, knowing that when you see that sun again, it will be on a day where there are no more battles to fight."

Everyone stood quiet. Even Archer's silence spoke volumes. For the first real time, they were looking farther than tomorrow. Up until now, they went from one fight to the other. They were good at it. They were made for it. They were dedicated to it. But what good would their efforts be if the world was still overrun by mutations long after their deaths?

For the first time, the members of Raptor Pack considered the possibility that they were only putting off the inevitable.

Charity was the first to respond to Kilmore.

"I'll make that promise. It will take me a long time, but I think I can create an antidote of sorts—something that'll only target the particle and not negatively affect living organisms. And Howard can come up with some bat-crazy method of dispersing it worldwide. Even as I talk about it, I feel like a second-rate comic book writer trying to come up with some crazy solution for an equally crazy problem, but then again, this *job* is crazy."

"And *we're* crazy for doing it," Renee said. She raised her coffee mug in a toast. "Fortunately, we excel at crazy."

"That we do," Charity said. She turned to look at the general. "Why don't we do it? Blow the damn thing up. Just say, 'oops, I accidentally dropped the meteorite in the middle of nowhere, and somehow five bunker buster bombs landed on top of it.'"

Kilmore sniggered. "*That* would get me to retire. Specifically, I'd be forced to resign. You guys want to see someone else in charge of G.O.R.E. Sector?"

Raptor Pack went silent at the thought.

That, in itself, said the answer loud and clear.

No!

"What time do they want it at Granger?" Thomas asked.

"Ten hundred tomorrow," Kilmore answered. "We'll load it onto a chinook and ship it over. I want you guys providing an escort. If you don't mind, I'd like to ride with you."

Thomas smirked. "You're asking? You're the general, General."

Kilmore chuckled. "Alright, I get your point. Dr. Tate, you think your kitties will be good riding with the package?"

"Absolutely, sir," Howard said.

"Are they still going with 'whatever they call it' company for security?" Thomas asked.

Kilmore clenched his teeth and nodded.

All six of them knew the deal. Senator Yuel did not want people possibly reporting to the general of what was taking place in the facility. A few senators and congressmen spoke up about the issue, only to be shot down with the counterargument that G.O.R.E. Sector should devote its resources specifically on hunting and destroying monsters, and not guarding government facilities. Funny enough, they did not seem to want to use the National Guard for that either.

Thomas scraped his boot over the ground, gradually forming a devious plan.

"They said we had to deliver the thing. They didn't say how long we have to stay."

Renee smiled at that. "Hey, even *Firebird-Two* can undergo 'maintenance problems.' It can take as long as forty-eight hours to fix. Maybe longer."

"Long enough for a tour of the facility," Kilmore replied.

"You think they will let us in?" Charity asked.

"You? No," Kilmore said. "Me? Yes. Do I think I'll get the whole picture? No. But I can get inside and Howard can get us a nice little look at the rest."

All eyes went to the engineer. Howard beamed a white smile at the group, then disappeared into the MEAV M2. He returned with a small device pinched between his fingers.

"I call this the Mosquito." He let the tiny drone go. Like the insect it was named after, it buzzed in the air, barely noticeable to the naked eye. "General Kilmore can get into the complex. A few of these mosquitoes can ride inside one of his pockets. When he gets a moment, they can disperse. They can go through the ventilation systems and any other passageway they can find, and get us a more detailed look at the place."

"Maybe we can find some familiar faces," Thomas said. "Maybe that Moran guy. Or the executive from Brom-Caylen whom we saw at the *Scarlett Caldera*."

Kilmore's expression livened up a bit. "It's worth a try."

"Is it possible the facility's security system can pick up on any signals coming from those things?" Renee asked.

"They'll be bouncing off the general's radio frequency, which connects to ours," Howard explained. "If they pick up on it, they probably won't question it."

"Good plan, Doctor," Kilmore said. "Let's go with it."

"We can still drop a bunker buster on the rock," Renee said. "Turn that thing into dust and bury it under ten tons of rock." She clicked her tongue. "'Oh, no! I accidentally dropped a bomb on it… or four or five.'"

Kilmore pursed his lips and shook his head. "As tempting as that sounds…"

Thomas checked his watch. "Ten-hundred tomorrow morning, you said; that's a good haul from here to Arizona. We better get started."

Renee was the first to strut to the ramp. "We better make sure we're stocked up on fuel."

"The ion engines are self-sustaining for at least another four years," Howard explained.

Charity shook her head and put a hand on his shoulder. "You've known her for *how* long, and you still don't know what she's referring to when she's talking about fuel?"

Howard rolled his eyes. "Coffee. Of course." He pointed a finger to Thomas. "I'll leave that for you to inventory."

Thomas remembered the debacle from the start of the mission to Zil Nesans. "After last time? I'll never forget again."

CHAPTER 3

The ground rumbled from the RPG explosion. A huge plume of smoke burst from the apartment building where it had struck, raining bits and pieces of brick, clay, and wood onto the street below.

Corporal Mylo Noverre hugged the wall, using its corner to keep himself upright as he and his men ascended the stairwell. The target was on the fourth floor, not too far from where the blast went off. With Bravo Team approaching from the west end of the building, it was safe to assume one of Khurto Tbileti's men had suicide bombed one of the marines by firing the RPG at point blank range.

It was one more of over seventy U.S. casualties associated with the evil terrorist, and that was nothing compared to the number of civilians whom he had tortured and killed.

Mylo knew the Iraq War had no shortage of debate. Whether it was good or bad depended on who you asked, and this included the civilian population. Many of the locals were generally not pleased to have the Americans occupying their country. But those who suffered the wrath of Khurto Tbileti felt the opposite. They were grateful for the interference, hoping the yanks would put an end to the demon once and for all.

Today was looking to be that day.

Thanks to intelligence provided by allied groups in the region, the extremist 'Author of Death' was tracked to a tall apartment building in the northern part of Baghdad.

The squad had met fierce resistance on the ground level and had managed to fight their way into the building. Mylo himself managed to score two confirmed kills; one near the main entrance, the second in the lobby.

Things were getting hotter by the second, and the physical turbulence was putting the building's structural integrity to the test.

By the time Mylo's squad reached the third floor, another explosion went off. Frantic dialogue flooded the comms, with some of the voices echoing through the various holes and shattered windows in the building. Gunshots popped off nonstop, both from AK-47s and M1 Carbines, with the occasional sniper round.

"No way are we letting Bravo Team have all the fun," the sergeant said. "Pick it up, ladies. Move it! Go! Go!"

Mylo took point, his gear insulating his already overheated body. His undergarments, not having been changed in two days, were clinging to his manhood. The gloves were catching the hairs of his knuckles, and a few red lines had formed where the straps of the vest hugged his shoulders and ribs.

He turned the corner and began making his way to the fourth floor. The doorway had been blown off the hinges by what appeared to have been a grenade explosion. Standing in its place was a man in charcoal-colored clothes, wearing a brown bandanna, and holding an AK-47. He was firing into the hallway, not noticing Mylo until the muzzle of his M1 Carbine was pointed at him.

A double-tap put a round through his chest and another through his face, eliminating the threat.

He took the next few steps with caution, anticipating another insurgent appearing in the man's place. More gunfire burst from somewhere down the hall, with Arabic voices shouting as they retreated southward.

The objective was nearly complete. The enemy forces were dwindling, the remainder now on the run.

Mylo reached the fourth floor and checked the hallway. Pieces of ceiling and glass covered the floor. Civilians cried from behind locked doors, unable to flee, but resenting being trapped in the middle of a firefight.

A few bodies lay on the floor, all of which were Tbileti's men. The sergeant and a few other marines started checking them, making sure there were no surprises.

"Whoa!" the sergeant exclaimed after prodding one of the 'corpses'. The man, whose act of playing dead was figured out, extended a pistol in the marine's face. The sergeant managed to knock the gun to the side with the barrel of his rifle, accidentally redirecting it towards the team's medic. The pistol went off, hitting the marine in the left hip.

The sergeant popped several rounds into the enemy at point blank range, ending his life.

Mylo looked over his shoulder, halfway down the intersecting hallway which led south. Some of his team members assembled near the injured medic while the sergeant began providing instructions to the others to sweep the rest of the floor.

When his eyes met Mylo's, he shrieked. "Eyes forward, Noverre!"

Mylo turned to his twelve o'clock. Another insurgent was backpedaling into the hallway, retreating from rifle fire from another hallway farther west. He was momentarily oblivious to Mylo's presence, for he was focused on repelling Bravo Team.

For Mylo, it would be like shooting fish in a barrel. It was a shot ideal for even an amateur shooter. He still had half a magazine left and there was no cover between him and the target.

By the look of it, he was about to have his fourth confirmed kill for the day. He put his eye to the scope, marked the target, and squeezed the trigger.

Nothing.

Mylo's heart jumped into his throat. He was trained to recognize when his rifle had jammed. It had only happened to him once before, and that was in the safety of a shooting range. Here he was, with an enemy gunman just a few yards in front of him.

The insurgent saw him. Shouting in his native language, he pivoted.

Mylo dropped the rifle and went for his sidearm.

BANG! BANG! BANG!

An exchange of rifle and pistol rounds zipped through the hallway.

Mylo reeled backwards. The first round struck his vest. The second one cut through his abdomen, the third through his left knee. His enemy also fell back, having taken a few hits to the chest and neck.

Mylo had gotten his fourth kill, but at great cost. He hit the ground, feeling his own blood pooling around him.

"Man down!" the sergeant announced.

His teammates assembled around him, putting pressure on his abdominal wound.

"Stay awake, Mylo!" one of them shouted. "Don't you even think of drifting off… Damn it! Mylo! Wake up!"

***

Mylo woke up with a shudder.

He was in his apartment, surrounded by the same beige walls he had been trapped inside since being discharged. The sun was starting to peek from the east, meaning the time was roughly a quarter to seven.

Beside his bed was his wheelchair. It was a sight that was met with disdain from the Iraq veteran. Even more so was that of his atrophied legs. Having lost the use of them in the war, the muscular tissue had basically shrunk to his bones. He always wore long pants to obscure what he viewed as a pitiful appearance, but it did nothing to lessen the mental torment. The round that struck him through the abdomen had chipped his spinal cord, paralyzing him from the waist down. Then there was his left leg, which had been saved in surgery, as though that did him a lot of good.

Every morning, he went through the same merry-go-round in his mind. It was worse when he dreamt of the war. He had that son of a bitch insurgent in his sights. All it took was a stupid malfunction of his weapon to change his destiny.

A buzzing from his nightstand brought a glimmer of new hope.

Mylo flipped his phone over and looked at the screen. It was no surprise to see the contact name from which the call was coming from. The person knew he was always awake at a quarter to seven. Only when Mylo was sick did he deviate from that routine.

He swiped the green icon and put the device to his ear. "Good morning."

"Mylo. How are you this morning?"

"Ready for a change."

"I bet you are. You've been waiting patiently. Today is the start of the new job. Meet me at the airfield in an hour. Are you sure you're up for this?"

Mylo looked again at those skinny, useless legs of his.

"You know how I feel. It's *you* who should be answering that question. If this goes south, you could end up behind bars."

"I'm committed to this. If I wasn't, I wouldn't have fought so hard for you to get this job."

Mylo closed his eyes and nodded. "Thank you."

"Thank me if this goes as planned. Alright, Corporal. Meet me at the airfield in an hour."

"I'll be there."

Mylo ended the call and swung his legs over the side of the bed. Planting himself in his wheelchair, he looked across the room at a cheap suit and tie he had set out for himself.

Today was the big day. He wanted to make sure he was dressed for the occasion.

CHAPTER 4

Thomas stood at the port window of *Firebird-Two's* laboratory. The MEAV, as well as the two model ones traveling five hundred parallel to their position, were moving at one-hundred-and-sixty miles per hour, keeping pace with the Boeing CH-47 Chinook.

Inside that tandem-rotor helicopter was a specialized cargo hold, designed for shipping nuclear waste. In this instance, the standards were fit for delivering the X41 meteorite. It was encompassed in a cube made of lead, each wall being two feet thick, its 'lid' only able to be opened by an electronic key.

The captain was not the only one on edge. Archer was at the port gun, tirelessly watching the nearby vicinity should any hostile force attempt to intercept them. Like Thomas, he trusted G.O.R.E. Sector's ability to maintain secrecy; it was the other group whom he did not trust. Leaks often came from within, whether it be from the government itself or the various companies they had contracts with.

They were in Arizona airspace now. Granger Valley was twenty-six minutes away.

Twenty-six minutes in which the meteorite would remain in custody. The thought was nauseating.

Maybe Renee was right. We should just bomb the hell out of the thing.

"I knew I was making a good choice when I recruited you."

He turned to the sound of General Kilmore's voice. The general was seated near Charity's desk. He had spent much of the trip admiring the craftmanship of

Firebird-Two. It really was a flying laboratory and a war machine all in one, designed for long-range missions, in which Raptor Pack could literally live for months at a time. Considering the increased frequency of monster appearances, such an upgrade was proving necessary.

Charity spent her time going over various bio samples taken from past mutations. When she wasn't typing notes, her eyes were either in a microscope or at a computer screen. Howard was at his desk, going over the mathematics and blueprints for his many inventions, all with a sharp focus that could not even be broken by a sarcastic remark from his captain.

It was in observing his teammates that Thomas understood the meaning of Kilmore's statement. Like Archer, he lacked education in the ways of science, which forced him to lean on his primary strength—security and combat planning.

"You're too kind, General. But you'd probably rethink your choice had you seen me at the Army-Navy Game of 2016."

Howard sparked a smile and gave a thumbs-up, much to the captain's amusement.

"Just so you know, we still won that year," Thomas continued. "No thanks to me, though. Turns out, I can only wade through a swarm of guys if I have a gun in my hand."

Kilmore smiled. "Nobody's perfect." He held his hand in the direction of the captain's desk. "Take a seat, Tom. You're exhausting yourself by being so antsy. Have some of that coffee Renee had you stock the shelves with."

With a mild chuckle, Thomas obeyed his order.

"How are *you* not antsy, sir? We're relinquishing custody of the largest known sample from the meteor storm to people we know will not treat it with the proper amount of caution. In my mind, it's like we're handing over a nuke."

Kilmore nodded. "Trust me, I'm not pleased with it. But I cannot say I'm surprised. This was bound to happen sooner or later, whether it's Brom-Caylen or some other entity." He stood up to refill his own coffee mug. "Ever since the fall of the Ecclesiastes Intergalactic Meteor Storm of 2019, several different entities have been pouring their resources into collecting and studying samples of the particle. Back when we first met—the Wasp and Hornet Invasion of Ramsey County, Oregon—the truth of the mutations was made public. But make no mistake; G.O.R.E. Sector was not the only organization aware of the problem. Several different groups throughout the planet had been delving into the issue, and all of them wanted it kept quiet."

"Easier to keep secret agendas *secret* when the general public is oblivious to the whole thing," Charity chimed in, not looking up from her microscope.

"Needless to say, up until recently, nobody was able to produce anything of substance," Kilmore continued. "Brom-Caylen is the first, that we know of, to find any significant meteorite fragments related to the Ecclesiastes storm."

Thomas turned his eyes to the chinook. "And now, it's in the hands of Senator Yuel, and whomever he has backdoor deals with." His hand squeezed the handle of his coffee mug. "This is going to get people killed. I don't trust these people. Frankly, I don't trust anyone other than G.O.R.E. Sector."

Kilmore tapped his shoulder. "Nor do I, son." He looked over at Howard. "Those robot bugs of yours ready to go?"

Howard rose from his seat and opened a small metal compartment in the bulkhead. Inside were five of the tiny little robots.

He pulled them out and held them on an open hand, displaying them to the general and captain.

As Thomas stared at the things, he felt a headache coming on. He could not even begin to comprehend the craftmanship and electrical work required to even make a functional device that small that was capable of performing all sorts of different commands.

"Careful not to squish them, Doctor," he remarked.

"Nah, they're more durable than that," Howard said.

Thomas plucked one from his hand and held it between his thumb and index finger. True to its name, the thing actually resembled a tiny bloodsucking insect, complete with wings.

Curious, he applied a little bit of pressure.

Crack!

Thomas bit his lip, feeling three sets of eyes burrowing into him. For once, he was no longer consumed with angst regarding the meteorite, as his mind was flooded with embarrassment for crushing one of Howard's devices.

The look from the engineer was precisely what he expected.

Smiling awkwardly, Thomas handed it back. "Might be best not to use this one."

Howard, glaring, took the crushed mosquito. "And there goes a hundred-and-fifty thousand dollars."

Thomas swallowed. "A hundred-fifty grand? For that little thing?"

"This isn't like the drones you find at the supermarket," Howard said. "First of all, you think it's easy getting a functional item to be this small? And have it be able to transmit and receive radio signals, follow commands, and relay a video feed? All from a long range? It's not like we're gonna be operating them in our backyard with a *PlayStation* controller. We're gonna be a ways away. Not only that, they'll be deep underground, underneath God knows how many meters of earth and steel." He looked at the general. "That's where that relay device will come into play, sir."

Howard pulled out a small piece of metal and placed it in Kilmore's hand. To the naked eye, it resembled a silver bolt one would purchase from *Home Depot*. There were a few black dots on its sides, no larger than the head of a pin.

"When you get into the facility, place that near the entrance. *Inside* of the facility, but *near* the entrance. Can't emphasize that enough. There, it should be able to retrieve signals from the mosquitoes and relay them to us. If you place it outside, the barricade doors might be too much for the signals. Too far inside, and the relay device might not be able to transmit to us."

Kilmore nodded. "Takes me back to when I used to watch *Mission Impossible*. The show, not the movies."

"Was that back when there were only three channels?" Charity quipped.

Kilmore gave a tight-lipped grin, knowing he had just dated himself. Only his rank shielded him from a full onslaught of age-related jokes.

"It's all gonna happen to you guys eventually. Give it time. And you can only pray you'll be as good looking as me." He tucked the relay device into his pocket and extended his hand to Howard to take the remaining mosquitoes. "You sure those things will be okay in my pocket? As Tom demonstrated, they're not exactly as durable as you claimed."

Howard gave him a sardonic glance. "As long as you don't actually try and squish them like literal bugs, they'll be fine. Once you're inside and have the relay device in place, all you need to do is let them out of your pocket, and I'll take control from there."

"Just don't make it obvious what it is you're doing," Thomas added.

"They won't suspect a thing," Kilmore replied.

"Hope not," Thomas said. "Because if you can't pull off the Peter Graves' method of getting in and out without anyone suspecting a thing, I'm gonna have to lean into my inner Tom Cruise and save your butt."

"Whoa, wait." Now, Charity was looking up from her microscope. "You think they would detain a general?"

"Absolutely," Thomas said. "Hence, they're using private security. Senator Yuel has had no shortage of verbal conflict with General Kilmore. He'd probably be delighted to get him locked up."

"I'll second that," Kilmore replied. He tucked the mosquitoes in his left pocket. "Fortunately, this isn't my first rodeo. I didn't get to where I'm at thanks to my good looks alone."

Thomas smirked, and returned to his desk. "Hollywood'll never know what they missed out on."

CHAPTER 5

The Granger Valley Research Complex was cross-shaped in its surface design. Powered by its own nuclear reactor, it was thirty miles from the nearest populated area. The above-ground structure resembled a typical school, except comprised of modular segments. Half a mile to the northwest was the nuclear plant. In-between it and the research were two lanes of concrete road. Multiple service drives provided stable routes for authorized vehicles around the facility.

Its main entrance was on the southwest cross arm, stationed near a large parking area and landing strip. Part of that whole setup was a group of landing pads for helicopters to land on. Two security vehicles and a large truck awaited, anticipating the arrival of X41.

As General Kilmore watched the complex, he envisioned the beehive-shaped underground structure beneath it, as well as the long tunnels stretching in all directions. It was a cold war facility, not just used for research, but designed for sheltering prominent individuals in the event of a large-scale catastrophe.

A few men with flags waved down the aircraft.

Renee Larson, bemused by their efforts, lowered *Firebird-Two* to the landing pad. "I regularly fly amongst oversized organisms that want to eat my guts, yet, these guys think I need to be guided onto a simple landing pad."

"I seem to recall you crashing a couple of times," Thomas quipped.

It got the desired response. Renee, exclaiming "Ohhh!", sped the MEAV onto the landing pad, frightening the hell out of the two men with flags. They turned on their heels and sprinted for safety, the MEAV appearing to come in like a kamikaze. She switched on the vertical thrusters at the last moment, bringing *Firebird-Two* to a dead stop a mere six feet above the pad. From there, Renee gently touched it down and lowered the ramp.

She emerged from the cockpit, eyes locked on to Thomas Rodney as though lasing him for an artillery strike.

"I seem to recall one of those times was to save your ass. Remember when that giant snake was about to squish that cabin in Wisconsin, with you in it?"

Thomas smiled, relishing in the juvenile antics of getting under the lieutenant's skin.

The other two MEAVs touched down on separate pads. Their ramps lowered, and a small team of support troops filed out. From the M1 designated *Ambient Wonder* came Lieutenant Belanger, who went right to work giving commands to his troops.

Until the meteorite traded hands, it was still in the custody of G.O.R.E. Sector, and it would be handled with the utmost care. The chinook landed on a large pad designated for supply drops.

Thomas stepped outside and watched the unloading of the six-by-eight lead cube containing X41.

A black limo pulled up to *Firebird-Two*, escorted by two security vehicles with the label *Trident* on their sides. From the limo's back passenger door emerged Senator Yuel. He was dabbing his sweaty brow with a piece of grey cloth. His suit jacket had been discarded, the top two buttons of his white shirt undone, his tie loosened.

General Kilmore came down the ramp. "Senator." He didn't bother to pretend to be pleased to see the idiot.

"General," Yuel replied in a similar tone. He checked his watch. "Almost ten a.m. right on the dot. I gotta hand it to G.O.R.E. Sector; you guys are punctual."

Another man stepped out of the limo. He was in his upper sixties, sporting a thin mustache, was slightly hunched in his posture, and wore a white lab coat that was a size too big.

"This is the famous Raptor Pack?" he asked, looking at the team with a great deal of admiration.

"This is them," Senator Yuel replied. "With General Austin Kilmore, the head of G.O.R.E. Sector."

The scientist approached the general and extended a hand. "Thank you, General. My name is Dr. Martin Zarek. I'll be in charge of all projects and research pertaining to X41 and the injectable samples. I certainly hope I can be of service to you. By that, I mean that, maybe together, we can find a long-term solution to the monster crisis this planet has been facing."

Kilmore gave him no expression. His face was blank, veiling the skepticism flooding his thoughts. He shook Dr. Zarek's hand and watched the side door of one of the security vehicles open up. A small ramp extended from its side, consistent with the designs for handicap vehicles.

A man in a wheelchair came down. To the surprise of Kilmore and the members of Raptor Pack, in it was a man in a security uniform, complete with a Smith & Wesson nine millimeter pistol on his thigh.

He was a man in his mid-thirties, whose upper body was well built, but whose legs were clearly wiry underneath those grey trousers. He had lived with his paralysis for a few years now, drawing both pity and a sense of respect from the general.

The man in the wheelchair pulled out a radio and held it to his mouth. "Teams Alpha, Bravo, and Charlie, move in on Helipad Four. Loading teams, remain on standby for package delivery."

Just from overhearing his words, it was evident the guy was high up in the ranks of security, if not the department head. The Marine Corps tattoo on his right forearm gave an insight into the man's background and experience. That, and the fact he was in a wheelchair, gave Kilmore an idea of how intense that background might have been.

Kilmore watched as the security APCs rolled up. From each one came eleven armed troops. They surrounded Helipad Four, rifles pointed low, ready to lift at any point should trouble arise.

The transfer began. A crane extended from the truck and brought a hook to the top of the harness. It lifted the lead crate from the Chinook and lifted it onto the truck.

Three G.O.R.E. Sector personnel moved from the Chinook's ramp with large, metal boxes, containing the liquified particle samples.

Dr. Martin Zarek cupped his hands over his stomach, watching the transfer take place with great fascination. Watching the guy, one would assume he was witnessing history; something rivaling the raising of the American flag on Iwo Jima.

In Kilmore's mind, it was more like the first Zero planes approaching Pearl Harbor.

The crane lowered the meteorite crate onto the flatbed. Those three containers were handed over to Granger scientists, who walked to one of the APCs with some security personnel escorting them.

"That concludes our transfer," Senator Yuel declared. "Thank you, G.O.R.E. Sector, for your help in this matter. Rest assured, our scientists will gladly share any findings with you. After all, you need all the help you can get in figuring out ways to exterminate giant organisms that will appear in the future."

Kilmore shared a glance with Thomas. For a split-second, he worried that the captain would not be able to hold his tongue. At the very least, the look on his face laid bare the expletives which were soaring through his mind.

Yuel offering well wishes and a desire to work with G.O.R.E. Sector was laughable at best. At the founding, he was one of the people who fought against them. He tried to micromanage their operations, insisting General Kilmore report to the Senate and House of Representatives for authorization for every operation. As the general pointed out, had things worked that way, the civilian casualty rate would be ten times higher. He was also the leading voice on preventing the public from learning about the mutations. When General Kilmore went to the news, Senator Yuel's first response was to demand his resignation.

Since then, he had been a burr in Kilmore's side on a consistent basis. Most of the time, the general came out victorious. It made the defeat over custody of X41 all the more painful. Of all the issues President Hudson caved on, this was probably the worst.

"Technically, the transfer is not complete," Kilmore said. "I cannot leave the meteorite until it's physically inside your building."

Yuel sneered. "Oh, for godsake…"

"*That* is the conditions of the transfer," Kilmore added. "Plus, I was hoping to get a look at your place." He turned his eyes to Dr. Zarek. Knowing Yuel would never agree to a tour, Kilmore hoped to appeal to the researcher's better nature. He did not know him well, but Zarek did appear to be more agreeable.

Then there was the security guy, who was a bit tougher to get a read on. Like Zarek, he was watching the X41 crate with dedicated eyes, entranced as though some mystical force inside had him in hypnosis.

"You'd like a tour?" Dr. Zarek asked. "Just for curiosity, or...?"

"Let's be real," Kilmore said. "Senator Yuel has probably told you already about how the big mean monster hunters did not want to share the meteorite. Personally, I'm worried about the security ramifications; not just for the storage of the samples, but containment for any test subjects that may get exposed to the particles." He watched how Dr. Zarek's jaw parted in angst at the mention of test subjects. "Yeah, don't bother denying it. I know that's gonna be part of the research. Here's the kicker: there's not a damn thing I can do about it. That being said, I'd sleep better if I can at least get a look at the place. Maybe show me some of the security measures you have. I know G.O.R.E. Sector has provided some weaponry."

Dr. Zarek looked over at the man in the wheelchair. "It's up to you, Mr. Noverre." Realizing the general was unacquainted with this individual, he went right to introducing him. "Forgive me; General Kilmore, this is Director Mylo Noverre. He's the head of security here at Granger."

Mylo offered his hand. "Pleasure's all mine, General."

"Likewise," Kilmore replied, accepting the gesture. "So, what do you say? Mind extending a little professional curtesy?"

Mylo gave a casual shrug. "Get in the Jeep. You can ride with us. Unfortunately, we can only show you the upper levels and some security footage of the sublevels. We have several areas that are off limits. Unless we get a direct order from the President, not even a man of your stature can be given access. I hope you understand."

"That I do. Much appreciated." Kilmore looked at his team members. "Hold down the fort. I won't be too long."

Thomas gave a sporty salute and returned to the interior of *Firebird-Two*.

General Kilmore joined Dr. Zarek and Director Noverre in the security vehicle. A security officer got in the driver's seat and started its engine.

Meanwhile, Senator Yuel returned to his luxurious limousine, not even offering Raptor Pack a hint of a thanks.

The vehicles moved to the facility's loading bay, where the transfer of X41 would officially conclude.

Thomas raised the MEAV's ramp. "Howard, get those monitors up and running. It's showtime."

"Got four screens ready to go," the engineer replied. "Technically, five were ready, but as of twenty minutes ago, one of them won't be necessary."

The rest of the team chuckled at the captain's expense.

Thomas grimaced. "I'm not gonna live this one down for a while, am I?"

CHAPTER 6

Now that he was away from Senator Yuel, Kilmore found the atmosphere a tad more pleasant. Dr. Zarek, as eccentric as he appeared to be, appeared to be a nice enough guy. Then again, Kilmore had encountered more than his fair share of individuals who started off pleasant, only to reveal their true colors later on. Given his fascination with the Granger Valley Research Facility, the general suspected there were some darker shades underneath the doctor's vibrant exterior.

Their vehicle pulled up to the compound's main entrance. Several security personnel awaited them, one of which came up to the driver's side door for the usual check-in procedure, even though the vehicle technically never left the property.

"It's quite an honor to have you here, General Kilmore," Dr. Zarek said. "Personally, I'm inspired by the many great things you have done with your organization. The scientists working under me are also fans of yours. You and that team of yours are regarded as heroes."

"That's very kind of you," Kilmore replied. "I would agree about Raptor Pack being heroes. They're the ones always doing the heavy lifting. Me, I'm more of a pencil pusher than anything else."

"No, sir," Director Mylo Noverre joined in. "Trust me, I've seen the stuff they've done. They would only be able to do their job so efficiently if they had a commander who had their back. Believe me, I know the difference."

Kilmore looked at the disabled head of security. "I appreciate that, son." He nodded at the tattoo on Mylo's forearm. "When were you in?"

"Oh-eight-to-thirteen." Mylo had a hand on one of his knees as he spoke. "We were after a high-value target. Twice, we had ample opportunity to take him down. One of those times could've been with a drone strike. But no. The colonel in charge of our battalion was indecisive. He was worried more about going after the target in populated areas. The thing is, he was playing right into the guy's hands. That delay allowed him to execute several strikes on convoys. After a helicopter was shot down, we were finally given the green light to go after him."

"And you were shot?" Kilmore asked. It was more of a statement of fact than a question.

Mylo rolled his jaw, reliving the memory.

"My gun jammed. The son of a bitch was right in front of me. I had him in my sights. A ten-year-old could've made the shot. Squeeze, click... next thing I know, I take a round through the gut and knee. All because my weapon failed me."

Kilmore nodded. "I understand being pissed off about that. It's one thing to take a hit in battle. It's another thing when it could have been avoided altogether. I'm sorry that happened to you. For what little it's worth, young man, you have my respect for pushing forward and not letting it keep you down."

Mylo sat straight. "That's worth a lot, General. Thank you."

The vehicle arrived at its parking space. The side door opened up and the ramp extended to the concrete.

Mylo exited the vehicle first, followed by the general and Dr. Zarek.

In front of them was the large, half-circular entryway. Steel doors sealed the exterior with latches strong enough to prevent a freight train from breaking through. The walls were made with a mixture of steel and concrete, designed to withstand a direct hit from a crashing airliner.

It was a sight that gave Kilmore some comfort. Even with security personnel who he did not view as up to the standard of G.O.R.E. Sector, these exterior measures would make an enemy force struggle to get inside.

The comfort was limited, for he still did not fully trust the intent of the personnel working here.

"What kind of research do you hope to accomplish?" he asked Dr. Zarek.

The scientist gave a small laugh, as though having expected the general to know the answer for himself.

"Why, *everything*, of course."

"'Everything' is kind of vague," Kilmore replied. "The thing is, there might not be a lot to actually learn from the X41 sample, other than what other types of mutation can result from it. My experts were hoping to find a way to either reverse the process or develop an immunity, and hopefully put an end to further mutations once and for all."

"I completely understand, General," Zarek replied. "No offense, but do you think I am going into this blind? You think I have not done any field research prior to being assigned to this complex?"

Kilmore gave that point some thought, then shook his head.

"Fair enough, Doctor. You mind telling me some of your background? I understand you might not have clearance to give away all of it, but if I can get any tidbits…"

"I don't mind at all, sir." There was a higher pitch in Zarek's voice, like a professor ready to speak in front of a new class full of students for the first time that semester. "Originally, I studied the effects of fusion particles on deep-sea organisms. You see, miles down, we believe there are radioactive elements. That company, Brom-Caylen, believed the same. They searched for tritium. I don't work for them, but some of my work did lead to their underwater excavations, because I helped identify deposits in some of the deep trenches. Personally, I was more interested in the sea-life that lived near the deposits. Some of them were close enough to be affected by the radiation, but to my amazement, many of them proved to be highly resilient."

Kilmore, to his own surprise, was intrigued by what he was hearing.

"Is that right?"

"Oh, yes," Zarek continued. "As you well know, we haven't even discovered all of the lifeforms in the deep oceans. But what I personally have discovered is that some of the species down there have immune systems we can barely even begin to comprehend. They can survive intense radiation. Maybe, just maybe, they can survive exposure to something else."

"Like the Ecclesiastes particle."

"That's right, General. In the past few years, I've been on my own field expeditions, searching for grains of the particle. With most of them being so tiny... literal particles... it was not easy. But time and dedication paid off, and we were able to locate some samples. Our first experiments took place here, in the sub-levels of this facility."

Kilmore perked up, not expecting this bit of information. "You've already performed tests on live animal subjects?"

"Can't make progress without doing so," Zarek replied. "Your people, too, would eventually have to resort to such measures if they hope to develop a cure."

It was a statement the general could not argue against.

"What animals?"

"A few species of fish collected from the deep sea trenches in the South Atlantic and Pacific Ocean. One of them, a translucent species I have named the Gorgo fish, was exposed to a whole grain of the particle."

"And it did not mutate?"

Zarek beamed a smile. "That's correct."

Kilmore stood quietly, analyzing the words he just heard as well as the man who spoke them. A rule of thumb was to not take anything at face value. He had only known this Dr. Zarek for ten minutes. For all he knew, the guy was making this up as he went along. Kilmore's instinct, on the other hand, informed him that what he was hearing was true. And if it was, it was groundbreaking.

A small part of him suddenly felt inferior. All of the funding and groundbreaking research G.O.R.E. Sector had done, and they had not gotten anywhere close to finding a treatment for the mutagen.

"Do you have any specimens here?"

"In one of the labs," Zarek explained. "It was not easy to catch them, let me tell ya. But we have three specimens, as well as a barn full of test animals."

This was the part that worried Kilmore; not the testing on animals, but whether the security teams would be able to contain any mutations resulting from the experiments.

"I don't imagine you're just gonna willy-nilly expose test subjects to the Ecclesiastes particle. Not without a plan in mind. With that in mind, am I right to assume you've developed some sort of treatment? A serum? Something to prevent mutation?"

Zarek was grinning as though he had just won a prize. He opened his mouth to speak, but held back for a moment.

Kilmore recognized the body language. He was limited in what he was allowed to disclose, but had the giddiness of a child eager to impress the adults around him.

"We have something in the works," he finally said. "It involves fluid from a lateral vein in the Gorgo fish, which runs parallel to their spinal column. The fluid acts as a natural bioluminescent marker, mostly designed for attracting prey. Additionally, it also works as a repellent. It can be expelled from a pore near their nostrils, creating a literal flash that can deter predators. We believe it can either avoid, or otherwise, *reduce* the mutagenic effects of the Ecclesiastes particle. Maybe, it will allow us to develop a perfect combination."

Kilmore cocked his head back, not sure if he liked the sound of that last sentence.

"What 'perfect combination'?"

"Something that would allow us to harness the benefit of the particle, but undo the negative characteristics. Namely, the aggressive tendencies that come with it." Zarek, sensing the general's lack of enthusiasm for his goal, turned his attention to the truck carrying the X41 meteorite. "Looks like our boys have transferred the package to the loading bay."

Mylo got on his radio. "Take the package to Sublevel Three."

"Copy that."

Mylo watched the general's face as he watched the bay doors seal shut. Behind them came a sound of droning gears as the freight elevator took the meteorite deep underground.

"Obviously, you're still a tad nervous," he said. "Feel free to come inside. We'll give you a little tour of the upper floor and show you how locked down this place is. Rest assured, nothing's getting in or out."

"Much appreciated," Kilmore replied.

Together, the three men approached the main entrance.

Mylo scanned his card and put his eye to the scanning device. The computer performed his retina scan and flashed green.

One of the doors unlatched and swung open, revealing a well-furnished entrance lobby. There were two security stations on both sides of the hall, both manned with at least one guard. They were fully closed offices, with a rectangular viewing port. It was more than a check-in area; these guys were expected to hold their ground here in the event of an armed incursion.

One of them stepped out at his director's request. "How can I help you, sir?"

"I need a guest tag for the general," Mylo said to him.

"Absolutely," one of the guards said. He went behind his desk, returning a moment later with a black lanyard clipped to a silver card. "General, sir. Here you go."

"Thank you," Kilmore replied. He waited for the guard to turn his back, and glanced over at his hosts. "I suppose we go straight ahead."

"Follow us," Mylo said. He wheeled himself forward, with the doctor at his side.

General Kilmore went to put the lanyard around his neck, then 'accidentally' dropped it by a small alcove in the wall. He knelt down to pick it up, placing the small bolt near the edge of the carpet.

He stood up, lanyard in hand.

The guard poked his head through the doorway. "Everything okay, sir?"

Kilmore sported a smile and lifted the lanyard. "Butterfingers."

The guard gave a smile and a thumbs up, then returned to his seat.

Kilmore caught up with Zarek and Mylo. They took a left at the end of the hallway. At the bend, the general noticed a couple of vents. It was the perfect place to unload the second part of the plan. And with no eyes on him, it was the perfect moment to dig them out of his pocket.

If anyone saw him on camera, it looked like nothing more than a man fixing his pants pocket, or, at most, pulling out lint. He let the tiny machines fall to the floor, not daring to look down at them as he followed his escorts to the next security post.

***

"He did it," Howard said. "The relay transmitter is in place near the entrance and the mosquitoes are deployed." He typed a few codes on his keyboard, activating the four super-miniature drones.

Four camera feeds appeared on his monitors, with a fifth one noticeably blank.

"Though we have access, it's gonna take a while for the drones to find their way through the facility," Howard continued. "If only we had a fifth one to help with the workload…"

Thomas made a tight-lipped smile. "I promise, I'll never touch one of your toys ever again."

"Yeah right," Howard quipped. "I might have to equip them with a shock device of some sort. Tase anyone that touches 'em."

"Or have them inject a sedative, or something," Renee added. "I mean, they're mosquitoes. Might as well live up to the name."

Howard raised a finger. "Not a bad idea, Lieutenant. And, since we know where the captain sleeps, commencing the strike should be as easy as boiling a block of ramen."

"Great," Thomas muttered. "Looks like I'll be sleeping with one eye open from now on." He extended his hand to the computer monitors. "What's the next order of business?"

"For bots One, Three, and Four, they'll go through the vents and air ducts and find their way into the sublevels. As for Two, he's gonna get into the security mainframe, where I'm going to hack into it and access all of their feeds and logs. And they won't suspect a thing."

"You sure their system won't detect an intrusion?" Thomas asked.

Howard tapped a few keys, directing Mosquito Two back to the security stations at the main entrance. "Not from these bad boys."

Thomas watched the POV from Two as it buzzed like a literal insect to one of the security stations. It found a place to land on the outer wall, then scurried to the edge of the doorway.

The guard inside was busy entertaining himself with a crossword while listening to a podcast on his phone, completely oblivious to the tiny robot entering his office.

"Alright," Thomas mumbled. "What's next? Wait for him to punch in his security code?"

"That could take forever," Charity said. "Especially since the computer is not set to go to sleep. At this rate, we'd have to wait until shift change when the next guy logs in."

"While that is part of the plan, there's also a quicker method." Howard waited to make sure the guard's face was turned away from the computer, then flew the drone to one of the vents on its side.

"Son of a—"

Raptor Pack went stiff, believing their little stowaway had been discovered. The guard slapped his neck, then looked at his hand.

"Everything alright over there?" the other guard said through his comm.

"Yeah. Damn mosquito bit me right on the neck. Got me good, too."

The five team members slowly exhaled in relief, the engineer giggling at the irony.

"That's the first time I've ever been grateful for one of those little buggers."

The bug's mechanical counterpart crawled inside the computer. There, it scanned the internal components, eventually locating the CPU.

Using a microscopic needle like a proboscis, it connected to the facility's mainframe.

"And, we're in," Howard declared.

On his secondary monitors, a slew of files and logs came through. Emails, personnel profiles, work orders, security logs, video feeds, administration schedules, and so much more poured into their hard drives.

Howard's enthusiasm gradually subsided. "That's a lot of stuff to look over."

"Your computers can't do it for you?" Renee asked.

Howard shook his head. "I mean, they can break it down based on keywords, access codes from specific individuals, and a few other factors. But all in all, there's still gonna be a lot for a human eye to look over."

Thomas tapped Charity and Archer on the shoulders. "Looks like the two of you have something to do while Howard's bugs comb their way through the sublevels."

Archer, per his usual self, was indifferent. Charity, on the other hand, gave a sour look.

"Oh, gee. Imagine my delight." She pointed at Howard. "Why can't he do it?"

"He's busy controlling the mosquitoes," Thomas said.

"Ah!" Renee filled a fresh cup of coffee. "Feels good to be the pilot."

"Oh, don't worry," Thomas said to her. "Once we find a place to set down, you'll get to join in."

Renee stood motionless, wishing she had kept her mouth shut. "To think we vouched for you to become the team leader last summer…"

CHAPTER 7

In the hours following General Kilmore's return from his tour of the Granger Valley Research Facility's surface level, *Firebird-Two* had remained docked on a hilltop four miles southeast. As expected, they were quickly detected by the station's security drones, and given an inquiry from Mylo Noverre through the radio. Following the plan, Renee informed them there was a minor engine mishap that was being worked on, and how they would be back in the air shortly. Mylo was kind enough to offer to send maintenance crews, but Renee assured them they had the best people on it already.

It was enough to make General Kilmore feel a tad guilty for the espionage Raptor Pack was engaging in. But there was more at stake here than good manners. The fate of countless lives depended on whether or not X41 was truly safe in the hands of Trident.

Renee's coffee supply came in handy, as the general and the five team members combed through the data they managed to hack, while also monitoring the feeds from Howard's mosquitoes. As they made their way through the sublevels, they created a map on the MEAV's computers, providing a detailed layout.

Shift change occurred at sixteen hundred hours. Most of the functions in and around the complex were standard. The administrative staff worked until five or six o'clock before departing. Helicopters came and went, acting as shuttle services for the personnel.

During shift change, the second-in-command of the security department, Drey Whiteford, arrived on site.

Thanks to Raptor Pack's access to the company files, they were able to identify him easily. He had spent four years in the United States Army, one of those years spent in Libya. From the audio and video feeds they watched, he seemed to be a reasonable man, not hot-headed towards his crew, and having their genuine respect.

As evening approached, Mylo Noverre and Dr. Zarek remained in the facility. The security director, from what they could see, was busy performing his usual tasks, routinely meeting with Mr. Whiteford and going in and out of his office.

Patrol vehicles roamed the service drive, occasionally parking and monitoring their designated side of the property. Drones performed their flights at random times, giving Mylo's crew a bird's eye view of anything taking place outside of the perimeter.

It was what was occurring underground that interested Kilmore the most. The mosquitoes took a while to find a way to the sublevels without tripping any alarms.

Watching their feeds was almost like watching old footage from deep-sea submersibles. They were slow moving, being so small, and the quality of the footage was grainy. All in all, it got the job done.

Sublevel One contained the clinical labs, several diagnostic testing labs, a biochemical genetics lab, cold storage, basic research, applied research, and some biosafety areas.

All of the equipment was top of the line, with at least one staff member in each room even in the later hours of the day. During the main hours of operations, there were countless science staff moving about, all oblivious to the mechanical insects watching them from the ceilings.

Sublevel Two was where things really got interesting. Unlike Sublevel One, which was essentially a maze of high-tech science rooms, precisely what one would expect to see, Two more closely resembled a maximum security prison.

It was going on twenty-hundred hours when Mosquitoes One and Four infiltrated Sublevel Two and began mapping it out.

There were some laboratories, particularly molecular genetics and agricultural, but what really had the team's attention were the various holding cells. One of the rooms had the aquarium Dr. Zarek had told Kilmore about. The drone moved in close to get a good video shot of one of the creatures behind the glass.

They were otherworldly in appearance, their bodies so translucent, they were nearly invisible. A purple lateral line ran from their snouts down to the back of their eel-like tails. Their eyes were a faint green color, their mouths lined with needle-thin teeth.

In the other aquariums were other marine specimens, including various species of squid, some sharks, crustaceans, bony fish, and eels. Pipelines and filtrations systems kept the water clean and oxygenated.

"So, this is Dr. Zarek's proposed solution to the mutagen," Thomas said. "A bunch of fish?"

"It's not out of the realm of possibility," Charity said. "We've always turned to animal and plant life to develop pharmaceuticals. We even use fungus to develop drugs. It's one of the reasons research is so important."

Thomas could sense a hint of bitterness in her voice. He knew precisely what was on her mind. For years, whenever she was not saving the world from monsters, Charity was working diligently to do exactly what Dr. Zarek was working on in Granger. She was pleased to know the scientist had gotten some small result in discovering an organism that reportedly could withstand exposure to the particles. Behind that optimism was jealousy. It was not ego; she did not want accolades for being the first to discover something so important, but Thomas knew she felt she owed it to her late husband.

Howard kept the mosquitoes exploring.

One of them passed through a long tunnel leading from the aquarium to another large chamber. It was a utility area, full of pipes and metal tubes, interlapping like a bowl of giant spaghetti noodles.

From there, the mosquito drone passed through another tunnel. At the end was a set of reinforced steel doors. Near them were elevator doors. As Howard scanned the area for an access route to get into the next chamber, those elevator doors opened.

Stepping into the tunnel was Dr. Zarek, walking with four other scientists and a man in a black suit.

"Is that who I think it is?" Kilmore asked.

"Zoom in on that individual," Thomas said.

Howard did the best he could. The signal was grainy, thanks to the layers of granite, steel, and insulation between the drone and the relay transmitter.

"I can't get a clear facial scan unless he looks directly at the camera," Howard said.

He turned to another computer he had set up, which had access to the facility's security feeds. He sorted through the sublevel cameras, eventually finding the one near a place labeled as *Canine*.

Thomas and Kilmore saw it too, and had the same nervous reaction as Howard.

Those doors slid open after Zarek swiped his key.

Howard took advantage of the opening, directing his drone into the chamber while the staff stepped inside.

The machine hovered high near the ceiling, granting a wide view of the laboratory.

It was maybe two hundred feet wide, hexagonal in shape, with three deep pits spaced out in a triangular formation.

Howard looked through the station's cameras, still unable to get a good view of the suited man's face.

"Dang it. I can't get a look at him."

"Can't you zoom in?" Renee asked, looking up from her laptop, on which she looked through an endless list of files.

"Technically, yes," he replied. "But that would tip them off that we've hacked into their system. I can look through some of their files. I was able to download stuff from the security guard's computer without him noticing. All we're really doing is looking at stuff that's available in the mainframe. But if I wanted to, say, move their cameras or zoom in, etcetera, that would be direct tampering. Meaning, they would pick up on the fact that, 'oh, hey, somebody took our camera off its automated panning system and is now zooming in on so-and-so. We might have a security breach.'"

Renee turned her eyes back to her computer. "Fair enough."

"What about sound?" Thomas asked.

Howard twisted a knob to amplify the signal. Voices came through the speakers, though staticky.

Dr. Zarek was in the middle of speaking. Unlike his time spent with General Kilmore, he was not upbeat. As a matter of fact, he sounded forlorn.

"I know this is what you want us to do, Senator."

Kilmore inhaled deeply. Just as he had suspected, the man in the suit was Senator Yuel.

"The question is timing," Zarek continued. *"We only just retrieved the meteorite. Believe me, nobody wants to conduct these tests more than me. But I need to fine tune the serum's regenerative process, and see*

how it reacts to human tissue before we can proceed further."

"It's been two years, Doctor," the senator replied. *"My people have been down my throat, demanding results. If I go back now and tell them we have to delay further because of safety concerns, I'll be drawn and quartered. You wanted more particle samples; now you've got a lifetime's supply. I want tests performed TODAY."*

Dr. Zarek shook his head. *"Though I have no doubt your sponsors and directors are breathing down your neck, I know that's not why you're in such a rush. You want this done because you want to know if—"*

Yuel raised a finger to the edge of Zarek's nose. *"Doctor, your work has been beyond valuable. But don't think for a second I won't find somebody to pick up where you left off."*

Zarek said nothing.

Watching the way he stood, both hands on his clipboard, the man was not only staying quiet to protect his job. He had the look of a man who wanted to make sure he did not end up in one of those holding cells.

Without saying anything else, Senator Yuel exited the chamber.

"Money talks," the lady scientist said to him in an effort to alleviate the atmosphere with humor.

"More than money," Zarek replied. He took a breath, then gestured at the nearest chamber. *"Let's start the test."*

There was a sound of gears coming from each pit, as well as the ceiling. The floor of each pit lifted until it was even with the frames. From the far end of the room, a set of double doors opened. Into the chamber came two scientists, wheeling in three cages. In each one was a dog. They were all German Shepherds, all injured, deformed, and in the case of one, paralyzed.

All three of them bore scars consistent with injuries obtained during military service.

"They're performing tests on injured animals from a K-9 unit," Thomas said.

Each of the animals was placed onto one of the elevator platforms. A glass barrier was lowered from the ceiling and trapped each of them inside. There was a sound of pressurization, preventing even a molecule of air from either getting in or out.

The poor animals yelped and howled, unnerved by their situation.

"Sorry, guys," a remorseful Dr. Zarek said. *"But if this works, you'll thank me."* He turned to one of his colleagues. *"Prep the mixture."*

There was a whirring sound from somewhere above, as though a giant blender was in the middle of creating a huge smoothie.

"Ecclesiastes particle is mixing with the Gorgo solution," one of the scientists said.

"E is at twenty, G is at eighty," another said.

"Dispense aerosol," Zarek said.

From the top of each dome, a gas dispersed into the three chambers. The animals continued their protest, putting their paws on the glass in search of a means of escape.

After a few moments, the domes were completely fogged over, obscuring any view of the helpless animals.

"Alright. Initiate suction," Zarek announced.

The tubes went to work vacuuming out all of the air inside of the three chambers. New oxygen was fed inside, breathed by the three test subjects, who now lay on their sides, their feet twitching, their tongues extending from their open mouths.

"Talk to me, people," Zarek said. *"Give me readings. How are they looking?"*

"Number one is stable," the female scientist said. *"Blood pressure is normalizing... brain activity boosting. White count is elevating. I think it's working."*

"Same for Number two," another of the scientists said.

"What about three?" Zarek asked.

"Blood pressure's increasing," the female scientist said. *"White count is highly elevated. Long thoracic nerve and intercostal nerves are firing signals."* She looked up with glee. *"Doctor, I think it's working!"*

By now, Charity, Renee, and even Archer gathered at Howard's station to watch the miracle that was unfolding. The glass cleared and a light was shone over each test subject.

The paralyzed dog stood up. It scratched its back paws on the floor, refamiliarizing itself with sensations it had not felt in a long time. Those legs were weak, having atrophied from non-use, but they functioned.

The other ones began to pace around their little holding cells. Their scars and other visual deformities were gone.

"Did I see what I think I saw?" Renee asked.

"They..." Charity gulped, questioning her senses, "...*healed* the dogs."

Howard brought the mosquito drone closer to one of the glass barriers.

"No sign of mutation that I can see."

"Incredible," Charity exclaimed. "They mixed the mutagen with the substance derived from the deep-sea fish and created a serum that produces an accelerated healing process."

"Wow." Renee knocked on the bulkhead with her hand. "Those animals were exposed to the particle *and* didn't turn into raging beasts? I think we may have found our cure."

Charity shook her head. "Except *we* didn't find it. They did."

"Whatever the case may be, I think we can start planning our retirements," Renee said.

"Let's not get ahead of ourselves," Thomas said.

The lieutenant looked at him and pointed at the screen. "Um, Cap? Did you not see the paralyzed dog stand up and walk? Oh, and not turn into a hellhound?"

"Yes, I saw it," Thomas said. "It's only been three minutes since their exposure. I'm not gonna break out the champagne and caviar until we know for sure this formula works."

"Looks like it works to me," Howard said.

Thomas groaned. "Long term. How is it the gung-ho army guy is the one still skeptical of this new magic potion?" He looked over at Archer. "Sergeant? What do you think?"

Archer pulled a piece of jerky from his vest pocket. "I'm not going anywhere near those dogs without a bazooka."

Thomas stood tall, glad to have his position reinforced by the sniper. "That's someone who uses his brain."

"Uses his brain?" Howard said. "He's talking about using a bazooka on some puppies *in an enclosed space,* fifty feet underground!"

"Gentlemen?" Kilmore said, redirecting their attention to the monitors.

Senator Yuel was back in the lab, expressing his joy in Dr. Zarek's success.

"Congratulations. My faith in you has paid off."

"I appreciate it, Senator. I must insist we hold off on the next trial until we can observe the long-term effects of the serum."

"How long?"

Dr. Zarek thought about it. *"At least a month. Maybe two. This is our first test, and we need to be sure that there's no side—"*

"Bollocks. We don't have a month. Certainly not two. He's gone through enough hell. It's our fault he's in the condition he's in."

"Um, with all due respect, Senator, I don't take any blame. I had nothing to do with us invading that country. That's a government thing—one that wasn't popular, even then. I'm definitely not one that cut costs to his unit, forcing them to keep using weapons that were doomed to malfunction at some point."

The senator raised a finger again, shutting Zarek up. *"That's enough. We're doing this tonight. We failed him. Just as we failed many of our troops. It was his WEAPON that failed that day, rendering him a cripple. How many of our troops suffered the same fate? Not any more. We're going to make the ultimate weapon— our soldiers! We will perfect THEM. Going forward, we will never have to worry about weaponry, for our men in uniform will be perfect. Now, get your ass to Med/Lab Three and get started."*

Zarek was clutching his clipboard again, looking to his colleagues for a comforting word. None of them dared to speak against the senator.

"Okay, but we'll have to hold him down here for a month. For observation, I'm sure you understand."

"Yeah, sure. That's fine."

"Is HE aware of this? Of the risks involved? That we are bypassing some very important protocols?"

"Yes. I am."

The people on screen looked to the southeast entrance of the chamber as Mylo Noverre wheeled himself in.

Dr. Zarek approached him like a parent about to speak to a teenaged son who was about to make a very bad life decision.

"There's a reason we study long-term effects on new medication."

"I understand, Doctor. But, as you can see, your invention works. If these dogs were smart enough to know what you did for them, they'd be licking your face." He wheeled himself to the glass barrier and looked at the formerly-paralyzed German Shepherd. *"Look at him. This is incredible. You've done the impossible, Dr. Zarek. You've healed a BROKEN SPINE in seconds! This dog should only barely be walking with the muscle loss in his legs, but he's looking better by the minute. You know how long I've wanted this for myself?"*

"And you will have it. But I need to know if there's anything in the formula that I must fine-tune. Please understand—"

Mylo whipped toward him. *"No, YOU understand."* Zarek backed away, as though the Marine veteran would spontaneously spring from that chair and beat him to a pulp. *"I've been trapped in this thing for too long. You think I haven't thought about throwing myself into traffic? Or eat a bullet? People actually think I have it easy, getting disability checks, not having to drive myself anywhere, now being handed this high-level job thanks to my father."*

The occupants of *Firebird-Two* exhaled a collective gasp.

"Interesting…" Kilmore muttered.

"Dad?" Renee exclaimed. "Isn't Yuel married?"

"To my knowledge, he only has two daughters with his wife of thirty-eight years," Charity replied.

"Internet concurs," Howard said, lifting his phone to show off the internet's findings.

"Color me shocked," Thomas said. "The senator must've had an affair at some point. The illegitimate child joined the Marines, went to Iraq, and ended up in that chair. Somehow, he and his dad found each other; Daddy feels guilty, both about his support for the war, and not being there for his boy; now he's making up for it by making him whole again."

"He probably didn't qualify for human trials because of his mental condition," Charity said. "So, Senator Yuel got him in as head of security in order to give him full access to the sublevels."

"Seems like his plan worked," Thomas said.

They watched as Dr. Zarek, defeated in the argument, escorted his patient through the far set of doors. The mosquito drone followed the group down another long tunnel, passing a few junctures before arriving at Med/Lab Three.

"Geez," Renee said. "This place is like an ant colony."

"G.O.R.E. Sector has facilities like this as well," Howard said. "I know: I helped design them."

"And how would you rank Granger Valley?" Thomas asked. "You think they're capable of handling a threat?"

Howard scratched his chin as he thought of the most delicate way to answer. "In terms of repelling an outside force? They're doing pretty good. But tests like these, which could result catastrophically, should be done at an offsite location. It depends on the level of mutation, but there is an inherent risk."

"Those steel doors look pretty tough," Renee said. "They'd probably be able to resist heavy weaponry."

"For a while," Howard replied. "In terms of keeping a mutant locked down, it depends on the extent of the transformation. We've all seen the variations. Some creatures, while dangerous, are relatively easy to kill.

The hornet drones, for example. Big, tough, and mean, yes, but they're not going to get through those doors. But that reptile we dealt with on Zil Nesans? Probably a different story."

The crew arrived at Med/Lab Three. It was a facility designed for air-tight quarantine for patients with highly contagious, deadly diseases. Every holding chamber was cubed in shape, the patient granted two-hundred square feet of space, with a bed, a chair, television, several changes of clothes, magazines, and bathroom. An airlock was located on the front for meals and medications to be passed through.

All of them were empty. At the moment, at least.

The rest of the chamber had a mixture of white, grey, and other neutral colors. There was regular furniture placed in the middle, as though it was expected for the staff to hang out with the patients and chitchat through the microphones that were placed everywhere.

"This glass is bulletproof, correct?" Senator Yuel asked.

"That's correct," Mylo replied. *"If anything goes wrong, nothing's getting out."*

Charity cringed. "Clearly, this guy has not dealt with mutations."

"No, he has not," Kilmore replied. "He's blinded by his pain and misery."

"Perhaps we should intervene," Thomas said. "This is not a sanctioned trial. He's clearly been turned down by whatever medical board works for this facility."

"And tell them what?" Howard said. "'Hey, we were illegally watching through your camera feeds while going through your logs, and we saw you were about to do the very thing we were afraid you'd do.'"

"Doesn't matter," Charity said, pointing at the screen.

Two of the staff members took Mylo through a set of white doors. A couple of minutes later, he reemerged, dressed in a blue hospital gown.

They wheeled him to a class atrium connected to the side of his confinement room. They placed him inside and faced him forward before sealing the atrium. Even through the drone's microphones, they could hear the hissing as the glass chamber went airtight.

"Last chance to reconsider," Dr. Zarek said. He stood at the main desk on the north side of the large room.

"Either I die in here or I live a life of a man who should've died in Iraq," Mylo replied bluntly.

Zarek looked at the senator, who nodded his approval.

"Begin treatment."

Just as what had been done with the dogs, a set of tubes connected to the chamber's ceiling let loose an aerosol mixture of the Gorgo formula with the Ecclesiastes particle.

Within moments, Mylo Noverre disappeared behind a thick fog.

The other scientists began providing readings to Dr. Zarek.

"Blood pressure's rising," one of them said.

"AGH!"

"What is that?" Howard exclaimed, alarmed from the obviously painful scream coming from within that fog.

"If your spine was realigning in a span of seconds, trust me, you'd react the same way," Charity said.

The screaming intensified, during which Zarek repeatedly looked over at Senator Yuel. The senator stood firm, his hands clenching into fists as he witnessed the spectacle that was, all at once, beautiful and intense.

"I'm seeing nerve signals," the female scientist said.

"Brain activity is spiking," someone else added. *"It's picking up new signals from the lower extremities."*

The screaming stopped and a new sound took its place.

Laughter.

Lots of laughter, followed by a sound of triumph.

"YES!"

"Cycle's complete," one of the assistants announced.

"Initiate suction," Zarek said.

The fog was sucked out of the small chamber, revealing the subject *standing* in the middle of the four walls.

Mylo's feet were wobbly, but functioning all the same. He kept his hands on the handles of his hospital wheelchair to keep himself from toppling over.

He looked down at himself while wiggling his toes for the first time in many years. A bright smile came over his face.

He stood straight, embracing the sensation of being pain free.

"Dr. Zarek, you did it." He looked at the doctor. *"Thank you."*

Zarek nodded, more relieved than anyone to see the head of security in good health.

"My pleasure. Well, sir, welcome to your home for the next month or two. As you can see, there's a phone in there. Drey Whiteford is obviously aware that you'll be out of commission, but you should have little trouble running things from there while he performs the bulk of the legwork."

After the decontamination procedure concluded, a doorway allowed Mylo into his hospital room.

He *walked* inside, pushing his wheelchair.

"Hopefully you got some good streaming services in here," he quipped.

The group of scientists laughed.

"Spared no expense," Zarek replied. *"We'll be monitoring your vitals and taking regular blood samples. If there's anything you need, let us know."*

"Any chance we can get some exercise equipment in here?" Mylo sat on the bed and pedaled his legs as though on a bicycle.

"We'll get right on it," his father said. Yuel went over to Zarek, his demeanor the polar opposite of the raging storm it had been moments before. He took the doctor's hand and shook it. *"Congratulations. This is going to change the world."*

Zarek had a look on his face that gave many different answers. For the time being, he went with the one that was politically correct and safe.

"Thank you, Senator."

In *Firebird-Two*, Howard was stretching his left leg. "I wonder if they can help with my sciatica."

His captain was not amused. While the rest of the team, aside from Archer, was fascinated by what they had just witnessed, Thomas was growing increasingly uncomfortable.

"I want eyes on that thing at all times," he said.

Howard looked up at him. "But the mosquitoes and the relay transmitter have limited range. Once we fly out of here, there's no way their signals will reach us. Plus, those drones are the only ones of their kinds, aside from the prototypes I have in my lab."

Without skipping a beat, Thomas Rodney had an answer for the engineer. "Looks like we're pulling an all-nighter."

Howard sank in his seat. "Great."

"That's some engine trouble we're having," Renee remarked.

"That's right." Thomas turned to face General Kilmore. "Sir, I can get one of the other MEAVS to pick you up."

Kilmore shook his head. "Captain, I'd like to stay and see what happens for myself. Needless to say, we've been witness to some extraordinary developments. Should more occur, I don't want to find out through radio calls."

"As you wish, General," Thomas said. "On that note, I hope you don't mind our menu. Lots of instant noodles and canned goods. We're a group with many unique specialties. Regrettably, culinary services are not among them."

Howard twisted in his seat to object. "Hey! I can cook."

"Sure," Renee said under her breath. "You can cook, technically."

"And all of Raptor Pack was almost wiped out as a result," Charity added.

"That was not my fault," Howard replied. "Just wait until you've tried my pan-roasted Ris de Veau. Oh, it's delicious. You soak the sweetbreads in cold water, add a pinch of salt and lemon juice…"

"Thank you, but I think I'll stick with the noodles," Kilmore said.

Howard zipped his lips and went back to work monitoring Granger Valley. "Ya don't know what you're missing."

CHAPTER 8

Mylo Noverre felt like a new man. As the clock neared midnight, he felt more energized than ever. He had no clue if he would even fall asleep. The dopamine was supercharged, as was his appetite.

He paced around the room, awaiting the arrival of the night shift nurse. The doctor at the monitoring station seemed to have little interest in him at this point, more focused on whatever he had on his computer to kill time than his actual patient.

Mylo was not sure why, but he felt a gradual irritation growing towards that man. Consciously, he was not sure why.

Of course the guy's gonna watch some sitcom on his computer. What else is he gonna do? He's supposed to be at the desk all night. He's gonna need something to keep his mind occupied. Hell, I'm supposed to be sleeping right now.

At this rate, sleep was far away in Mylo's future. He tried lying in the bed a few times, but he couldn't remain there for more than a couple of minutes. There was too much energy flowing through his veins; too much excitement occupying his mind.

How could one not feel this way after receiving the miracle he was given? For too long, he had been trapped in that chair, feeling the pangs of his nerves firing false pain signals up his back. There were many nights that sleep was impossible, for no medication could dull the agony. At least tonight, the lack of sleep was from a good feeling.

Mostly.

Mylo passed his tray table for what felt like the millionth time, glancing at the three plates he had cleared off. He had requested an additional serving of beef stroganoff, mashed potatoes, steamed vegetables, and rice, and the nurse was taking her sweet time getting it to him.

Furthermore, they did not clear his dirty plates. Not that they were truly dirty—he had cleared them thoroughly.

As far as his stomach was concerned, he had never been fed at all. His body was burning fuel fast. His leg muscles were quickly regenerating. By now, he was walking with no difficulty.

A door opened on the opposite side of the room. Dr. Zarek entered and walked directly to the glass.

"I see you have a hell of an appetite."

"I can imagine worse side effects," Mylo joked. His fingers tapped on the glass as he spoke.

Zarek was looking at his fingertips, noticing the jittery way they moved, as well as the slight increase in girth. His eyes traveled the length of Mylo's arm, taking notice of the increased muscle mass.

"How's the exercise equipment? Is it sufficient?"

Mylo looked over his shoulder at the free weights and treadmill he had been given.

"They're okay. I need to get some extra reps in to get any sort of burn."

"I see." Zarek stepped away to join the other doctor at the monitoring station.

Mylo remained at the glass, fingers still tapping, watching him.

"How's everything looking?" Zarek asked the other doctor.

"You sure there wasn't coffee mixed in with your special serum, sir?" the doctor joked. "He's been up and moving for the last few hours. No sign of stopping. And eating like a hyena."

Mylo tapped the glass to get their attention. "On that note, where's the nurse?"

"She'll be here in a few minutes," the doctor said.

"That's what you said a few minutes ago," Mylo replied.

"We're literally cooking to order," the doctor said, not bothering to look up from his stupid computer screen. "Just be patient."

Mylo's fist came down on the tray table. "Don't tell me to be patient!"

Both scientists' eyes whipped to the patient and the section of oak wood that had been busted off the tray like cheap plastic.

Mylo looked down at his hand and the damage he had inadvertently caused. A sense of realization took over.

Slowly, he backed up to his bed and sat down, not daring to say another word.

He could hear the beeping of his heart rate monitor and saw the concern on Dr. Zarek's face. Now, that program on the other doctor's screen was switched off.

He leaned over to Zarek and whispered, "Should I alert Mr. Whiteford?"

Zarek nodded.

Mylo felt his temper starting to boil once more. The two bastards were talking about him as though he was not even here. Furthermore, they were concerned that he was a security risk.

Mylo Noverre, head of Granger Valley security, Marine Corps veteran, a man never arrested once in his life, is suddenly a security risk?

Another sense of realization gave him pause. The scientists were whispering, their microphones turned off, yet he could hear them through the glass barriers in front of him.

Dr. Zarek started going for the door linking Med/Lab Three with the chamber with the German Shepherds.

"I'll be back soon." Increasing his pace, he hurried into the tunnel.

In that moment, Mylo detected another sound.

A faint echo, like the voices of ghosts moving along the steel walls.

Shrieking. Yelping. Howling.
Snarling.

CHAPTER 9

Witnessing the interaction between Mylo Noverre and Dr. Zarek successfully lifted Howard from his slump. For the last hour, he had been struggling to stay awake. But this new development with Mylo got his heart pumping.

It was the same for Thomas.

"Keep an eye on that."

"You got it," Howard replied.

"Any news on the dogs?"

Howard shook his head. "They lowered them down into the pits. It's hard to get a good visual. The glass domes are still covering them. I can't get a good look. But I'll say this: something's going on, and it's making the staff nervous."

Thomas watched the body language of the scientists in the hexagonal chamber.

"Not just them."

"Hey, Thomas," Renee called to him. "You might find this interesting."

The captain moved to his desk where the lieutenant was seated. "What is it?"

"I found a familiar name on the log. You remember this?"

She moved aside for him to look at the screen. There, listed for Wednesday September 2nd, was the name Dr. Gretta Domergue.

Thomas' eyebrows slanted and his jaw clamped, recalling the moment he became acquainted with that name.

Zil Nesans, in the south facility. He remembered the letter he had found in her office before Raptor Pack was attacked by a pack of mutant reptiles, and later, the mercenaries led by Moran.

Hello Dr. Domergue. I have received your email regarding the specimen and have taken your concerns into account. The co-sponsors do not agree with your assessment, frankly, and they threaten to withdraw funding unless you go through with the project as planned.

If things get out of hand, have the security forces put the subject down. At least that way we can say we tried, and it won't look as if we're stalling. Our partners want to be assured that the stuff can at least yield results of some kind. They'll be able to tolerate if more tinkering needs to be done with the formula, but the endless postponement is giving the impression you are not confident in your theory.

Please run the trial by the 21st.

-   Harvey Q.

"General?"

Kilmore approached the workstation. "Got something, Captain?"

"We might have a link to Brom-Caylen," Thomas replied.

"At the very least, that operation on Zil Nesans," Renee clarified. "Technically, we did not find anything that truly linked those facilities to the company. They're keeping things close to the chest."

"True enough." Thomas thought about that letter he read on the island, fixating on the name at the end. "Harvey Q. Hey, Charity? You have the staff files on your computer?"

"I do."

"See if you can find any info for anyone with the first name of Harvey and a last name beginning with Q, will ya?"

"Q…" The biologist went to the alphabet icons for last names, clicking on the desired letter. "Alright, let's see what we got here… Fredrick Quarry… Martin Quinn… Lanette Quesada… yadda-yadda…" She stopped scrolling. "Harvey Quarter."

Renee went to work looking for any significant files regarding that name.

"It's fun doing detective work," she said, turning her laptop so Thomas could see the screen. On the page was a photo of a man in his fifties, wearing a blue suit and black tie. He looked like any other businessman in that age group, slightly overweight, showing faint signs of hair recession.

"Harvey Quarter," Thomas read aloud. "Senior Vice President for Brom-Caylen's pharmaceutical department."

"Bingo!" Renee snapped her fingers. "There we go. You have your connection to Brom-Caylen."

"Well done," Kilmore said.

Thomas was not giddy. If anything, he looked frustrated.

"*We* know. Problem is, we can't prove it. The letter was lost when Moran's group destroyed the South Facility, and there was nothing in the north one to give us any leads. If we go to anyone to start an official investigation, we'd be asked to produce the letter. When we tell them we do not have it, they'll chalk it up to hearsay." Sighing, he looked out the window in the direction of the facility. "I wish I thought to grab it. Now, we know Brom-Caylen is involved with Senator Yuel and is taking part in the experiments in those sublevels. They probably promised him all sorts of things, like curing his son of his disability. In return, he dedicated himself to getting them as much funding as possible. Probably one of the reasons he has been a pain in the ass of G.O.R.E. Sector; he wanted our funding to go to the company."

Kilmore looked over at Renee. "I'm starting to wish I had the guts to follow your advice; blow up that meteorite and prevent anyone from getting their hands on it."

Renee offered a comforting smile. "In fairness, General, that might've been a stupid idea. I mean, blow up a rock that is essentially a vessel for a dangerous particle, and risk dispersing it for God knows how far? A big container of acid would probably be better."

Kilmore smiled. "That's a very good point." He looked outside, thinking of the facility. "Or, wait until that place is emptied, and drop those bombs on it and bury that meteorite under sixty tons of rock and metal."

Charity whistled. "The government would have you drawn and quartered. Unless some major catastrophe took place in there, you'd have no grounds for launching that level of assault."

Beep! Beep! Beep!

All eyes went to Howard's monitor. The alarms came from the audio recorders from the mosquito drone in the containment chamber.

On the screen were several scientists scrambling for the control boards.

"Alert Dr. Zarek," one of them shouted. *"Gas 'em."*

"The senator will have us crucified!" someone else said.

"Do you not see what's going on in there?" The first scientist pointed at the three glass covers. *"I'm not betting my life on them not getting through that glass. We're gassing them."*

He turned a few knobs and flipped some switches. A blaring alarm went off, alerting him that the poison gas was ready to be dispersed in all three holding cells. A key was inserted into a slot, unlocking a lid covering a large red button.

Without hesitation, the scientist slammed his fist on it.

Three hissing sounds went off, and the glass domes began fogging over.

Charity put a hand over her mouth. Not being able to get a visual on the three dogs was driving her crazy, as her brain conjured up horrifying images of what was happening to them.

"The formula did not work," she said. "They still mutated. Only, the effect was delayed."

Thomas watched a feed from the surface station. Whiteford had received a call from the lower levels and got right to work suiting up in tactical gear. Every security guard on site, save for those at the entry points, rushed to the armory, where they grabbed extra magazines and high-powered assault rifles.

In large groups, they started going for the stairwells.

"Howard, switch the feed over to Mylo's room," Kilmore said.

The engineer brought up the feed.

Dr. Zarek had just rushed into Med/Lab Three as it appeared on the monitor.

"Give me his readings," he said to the two doctors at the monitoring station.

Mylo was at the glass wall. His gown was partially ripped. Behind him, the bed was ripped off the floor and knocked over. There were a few cracks in the wall, the television was knocked over, and the IV lines were torn from his arm.

"Blood pressure's skyrocketing. Sed rate's through the roof. Brain waves are all over the place," one of the doctors said.

Zarek started looking over the monitors. *"Whiteford's on his way down."* He picked up the phone. *"What's your status?... Did you euthanize them?... Okay, finish up, then clear out. Whiteford's leading a response team as we speak."*

"What's the idea?" a growling voice roared from the cell. *"Gonna shoot me? I've been shot before!"*

Stricken with horror, Zarek looked over at Mylo. The marine was on his hands and knees, keeping his face down. A huge bulge had appeared from his left shoulder, the flesh darker compared to the rest of his body.

"No. Mylo... the treatment didn't work. You're... you're... mutating!"

"It worked perfectly fine." Mylo stood up, revealing his increased height and bulkier frame. *"Go ahead. Gas me! Give it your best shot."*

In stunned silence, Raptor Pack watched the lead scientist fumble over the control board with his hands.

The phone rang.

One of the other doctors answered it, then extended it to Zarek. *"It's the senator."*

"I'm not available."

"He knows you're here."

Stressed out, Zarek took the phone and put it to his ear. *"I'm sorry, Senator. It didn't work. I have to engage the containment protocol... Even if the glass holds, we'd still have to deal with the threat. We don't know how to reverse it yet, or if it's even possible... No, Senator, I'm sorry, but I have to do this... I have to... Do what you have to do."*

He slammed the phone down and armed the gas lines. *"I'm sorry, Mylo."*

The cell filled with poison gas.

Mylo stood still, watching the scientist with unblinking eyes as his room fogged up. As he stood there, he grew another six inches, the twitching in his other shoulder and neck noticeable even to the people watching inside *Firebird-Two*.

In a few seconds, the cell was completely white.

The south doors opened. In came Whiteford and eight other security guards.

"I want a team in every tunnel and every room in the sublevels. If one of the specimens escape, I want every inch of this place covered. We can't risk letting them get to the surface."

"Can't they just self-destruct the place?" Renee said.

"And willfully bury billions of dollars of equipment and their grand find?" Kilmore said. "They would never entertain the thought in a million years."

Minutes passed.

Whiteford's men spaced out inside of the Med/Lab, weapons pointed at Mylo's cell.

"Okay, it's been long enough," he said. *"Doctors, siphon out the gas."*

After a few moments of hesitation, Zarek operated the control board and began suctioning the poison gas from the cell.

The fog cleared, revealing the interior of a trashed cell. In its middle was Mylo Noverre, lying on his side, huge hands tucked over his head.

"What are his vitals?" Whiteford asked.

"I don't know," Zarek replied. *"His lines have been pulled out. The computers can't get any readings."*

"That gas is strong enough to take down a herd of elephants," one of the guards said. *"He's got to be out cold. Being a mutant doesn't make you invincible."*

Silence followed the statement.

Following the silence was a gravelly laugh. It was low and barely audible at first. Little by little, it grew louder, Mylo's shoulder's bouncing as the laugh intensified.

As it grew louder, it got deeper.

Mylo pushed himself up on his two enormous hands. *"Mutants? No!"* He twisted his neck, his surface features misaligning before everyone's very eyes. *"Not invincible. But thanks to Zarek's pet fish, you'll need more than fumes to kill me."*

Zarek went into the middle of the room and put his hands out in hopes of deescalating the situation.

"Mylo, you're gonna be okay. Just stay where you are. We'll do whatever we can to get you back to normal."

The head of security put his grey forehead to the glass, revealing the crest that was forming around his hairline.

"Normal? I WAS normal. Normal was hell. I feel great!"

He threw his head back as his mutation progressed. He grew another several inches, his clothes ripping, his body swelling with muscle mass. His gown fell off completely, revealing a torso covered in thick skin with a gravelly texture. His arms had grown longer in relation to the rest of his body, similar to a gorilla's. His feet burst from his slippers, the toes pointed like arrowheads.

The waist of his pants fell free, taking his manhood with them.

Mylo Noverre was no longer human. He was a 'thing', free of gender or humanity, more related to a beetle than the human race.

His brain underwent its own alteration, erasing the human side, and turning him into a rampaging beast.

A huge fist struck the inner layer of glass, shattering it. The guards shuddered, taken off guard by the sight of the bulletproof barrier coming apart so easily.

Thomas looked to Renee. "Get us in the air."

She nodded and hurried to the cockpit.

At this point, they could not, in good conscience, remain uninvolved. Sure, they would probably have to explain that they hacked into the system, and that was how they knew things were going wrong. But the backlash to that was the least of their problems.

Mylo Noverre was a mutation. And like all mutations, he was possessed with murderous aggression that not even the human spirit could will its way out of.

On the screen, he struck the second layer of glass, ridding all separation between himself and those pointing guns at him.

CHAPTER 10

With a swipe of his mighty hand, the creature named Mylo widened the gap in the dual-barrier of bulletproof glass. He stepped into the room, sporting a sinister grin with razor-sharp, yellow teeth. They, like the rest of his body, had also changed in form; many of them now cone-shaped.

He stood at eleven feet, his skin rough in texture like a toad's, except much stronger. His forehead had extended over his orange eyes. Behind that brow were two narrow holes; the sole remaining feature of his ears.

Whiteford put his eye to his rifle's scope, centering that red dot over Mylo's chest.

"Mr. Noverre... Mylo! Don't do it."

Mylo rocked side to side, his veins bulging through that grainy skin. Even now, the mutation was progressing.

He growled in pain and leaned forward, allowing the spines to emerge from his elbow joints and shoulders.

"No do it?" He stood straight, his voice coming out like thunder from a raging hurricane. "No do it? Do it?" He smiled and made eye contact. "Do it!"

His next sound was a deep roar, reminiscent of colossal prehistoric beasts out for the kill.

Whiteford knew the deal; Mylo Noverre had descended into madness. The only thing that would stop him now was death.

"Open fire!"

All eight of Whiteford's men joined him in bombarding the mutant with an endless barrage of bullets. Mylo twisted and jerked, the bullets stinging his flesh. He stumbled backwards, hands instinctively placed over his face.

Crushed pieces of lead rained onto the white floor. Mylo lowered his arms, now aware there was nothing to fear from those guns but mild, annoying stings. His chest expanded as he took in a large breath.

The men reloaded and resumed firing, many of them planting bullets on Mylo's skull.

His head jerked back, the skin marked by the vicious impacts. Aside from those minor scrapes, he was effectively impervious to rifle fire.

Mylo panned his eyes across the large room, making eye contact with each and every one of the soldiers and scientists in the room. In spite of the whirlwind taking place in his crazed mind, he still recognized each one and remembered their names.

Taylor, Gaylord, Divino, Yate, Eckhart, Mallory, Cruger, and Keene. At the monitoring station were three scientists crouching with Dr. Zarek: Dr. Waker, Dr. Brom, and Dr. Abadi.

As a human, their safety was his top priority.

But Mylo was no longer human. What he was now lacked compassion and decency. It still felt joy, but only from charnel thoughts preceding worse intentions.

Some of the guards backed away, one of them muttering, "Oh, God."

Baring another smile, he began his retaliation.

In addition to improved size and strength, Mylo was faster and had a stamina professional athletes would kill for.

In the blink of an eye, Med/Lab Three erupted into chaos, quickly falling apart as the beast tore through the security team.

Divino was first to suffer his wrath. Mylo grabbed the guard by the shoulder and lifted him six feet off the floor. Kicking and grunting, Divino watched that other hand ball into a fist, pull over Mylo's shoulder, and come at him.

The impact crushed his chest and everything inside. He flew across the room and slumped against the wall, dead.

More bullets struck the beast.

Mylo spun on his heels and laid eyes on Gaylord and Cruger. The two men were at the security station, the latter yelling to the scientists to retreat into the hallway.

The beast moved in on the station. A swipe of his claw-like hand bashed Gaylord, knocking him hard against the back of the long desk. The guard's upper body snapped backward, folding him over one of the monitors.

Cruger pointed his rifle and hit Mylo between the eyes with a well-placed shot. For any other enemy, it would have been instant death. For the mutant, it was a pesky annoyance.

The guard was snatched off his feet, held by his legs, and whacked mercilessly against the floor.

"Run! Run!" Whiteford yelled to the scientists.

Dr. Zarek waved at his colleagues, guiding them to the east doorway.

Mylo, hyper-focused on the doctor, chased after them.

Dr. Brom found himself in his grasp.

"No! No! NOO!!!"

Mylo threw him at the controls for the doors, connecting his skull with the panel. Both his head and the control panel caved in, stopping Zarek from making an escape in that direction.

"This way!" Whiteford shouted to the doctors, pointing at the south doorway.

Mylo moved to intercept, only to take more shots to the face from the guards. Incensed, he delayed his assault on Zarek in favor of getting even with these puny humans in front of him.

He raised a fist and hammered it down on the top of Eckhart's head, caving it down into his torso.

Next was Keene, who stumbled backward after watching his friend get pummeled. His fate proved to be worse, as Mylo lifted him up, held his legs in one hand and his shoulders in the other, and gave a sharp twist.

Crack!

"AGH!"

Keene was dropped to the floor. He looked down at himself, seeing his own buttocks below the corkscrew of flesh and clothing where his spine had snapped. It was a trauma that also ruptured many internal organs, preventing him from a lifetime in a wheelchair.

"Fall back!" Whiteford said. He was standing by the steel doors leading to the south tunnel. The doctors were currently racing to the next chamber. Meanwhile, Whiteford and his two remaining guards were moments away from following them.

They did not move fast enough.

Mylo leapt several yards, catching Mallory in the middle of the room. His huge foot came down on the guard, driving him to the floor, where he was crushed to jelly.

"Oh, God!" Yate shouted, faltering a few steps from where Mallory's blood oozed over the floor.

"Move!" Whiteford shouted, now waiting on the other side of the door.

Yate's fear and hesitation was his downfall.

Mylo extended his jaws, revealing those horrible teeth. Yate was grabbed and lifted towards that mouth, squealing in anticipation of his nightmarish fate.

Whiteford, unable to help the guard and not wanting to witness his slaughter, sealed the door.

He heard blood splattering inside Med/Lab Three, and the *THUD* of Yate's body being thrown against the door.

Next came heavy footsteps, then *BANG!*

Whiteford jumped back.

Behind him, several troops approached with their weapons shouldered. The sight of the door bending inward gave them all pause.

"The hell?" one of them exclaimed.

Whiteford backed away. "Withdraw to Med/Lab Two. We need to lock this whole place down."

BANG!

Whiteford spun to face the doors, watching with astonished eyes as the steel barrier bulged towards them.

BANG!

The bulge expanded, the slit between the two doors folding outward. Through it, he saw the mutant stepping back, winding itself up for another strike.

"Oh, my god," one of the guards said. "Those doors are made of steel. They're designed to withstand an impact from MANPATS rocket launchers. And he's literally flattening it like a rusted segment of grid fencing!"

"Fall back," Whiteford said, his voice getting shakier by the moment. "Get out of here. Evacuate the entire—"

BAM!

The doors came apart with explosive force, their fragments bouncing into the tunnel.

Mylo threw his arms out, leaned forward, and bellowed at the frightened troops.

Gunfire echoed through the hall, their projectiles doing nothing but spurring the mutant further.

"Go! Go! Go!" Whiteford shouted to his men.

A few of them retreated, while others, stricken with fright, attempted to eliminate the threat with their weapons. It proved to be a fatal mistake for each of them.

The first was smacked off his feet and into the wall, where every bone in his body shattered on impact. Mylo pivoted to the right and grabbed ahold of another, holding him high before pulverizing his abdomen with a left-hand punch. He followed up the hit with a headbutt, crushing the poor man's skull.

Tossing the fresh corpse aside, Mylo lunged at another. A steady stream of lead struck his chest, doing little more than tickling him before making his next kill.

The soldier, either because of fright or macho stubbornness, held his ground even as the titan stampeded in his direction. His magazine went dry. Instead of making a run for it or switching to his sidearm, he raised the gun over his shoulder, and struck the mutant as he was grabbed.

Mylo, amused by the man's effort, easily pried the gun from his hands and held it like a hammer.

CRASH!

The soldier's body hit the ground, the head pulverized by a much heavier strike with his own weapon.

Stepping over him, Mylo identified his next target. Most of the soldiers were making their retreat to the next chamber. Two guards at the rear of the group backpedaled, providing cover while the rest retreated.

Baring that sinister grin, Mylo raised the dead guard's gun. His Marine Corps training flashed in his demented mind. For a split-second, he was on the field, practicing throwing knives. By the end of the week, he had managed to nail the tip of the blade directly between the eyes of his cardboard target.

Using that same motion, he threw the gun.

The target was knocked off his feet, the edge of the stock striking him right between the eyes. He hit the wall, spun once, and faceplanted, trickling blood from his nose and ears.

The success of the tactic brought a ping of satisfaction to the mutant. As it turned out, Mylo Noverre did retain one aspect of his humanity.

The worst aspect.

The thrill that came from killing another human.

It was a feeling that flooded the creature's foul mind, growing more potent as he moved in on the other guard.

Mylo straightened his hand and fingers. Another technique came to mind, not from his days as a marine, but his teen years practicing karate. A spear hand technique. It was exactly what it sounded like; a direct strike with the fingers locked out, *spearing* the opponent in the throat or eyes. Personally, Mylo never found the technique useful, for he felt he would more likely break his fingers than do any damage to an opponent.

But with his new augmentation and desire for murder, that was no issue.

The air was driven from the guard's lungs, his arms and legs twitching as he was lifted up, the mutant's fingertips protruding from between his shoulder blades.

Mylo angled his hand down and let the dead man slide off his fingers. His eyes went to the rest of the group.

He recognized the path, for countless times he had patrolled, inspected, and assigned posts for every inch of this underground facility. Though transformed, his memory remained intact, as did his knowledge of this battleground.

They were heading for Med/Lab Two. Beyond it was a small room for vending machines and elevators. Undoubtedly, that was where Dr. Zarek was trying to escape to.

Mylo had his destination. Even if he did not catch Dr. Zarek in time, he knew where the scientist would run to. The doctor had attempted to murder him with gas and had called armed security troops to end his life. The logic of the situation meant nothing to Mylo. He had exactly what he needed—an excuse to *kill*.

He pursued the troops to Med/Lab Two with intent to do exactly that.

CHAPTER 11

Firebird-Two hovered over the southeast lot, bypassing the landing pads and set down thirty feet from the building's main entrance. Multiple security personnel were standing outside, all of them fully armed, as the site had become an active warzone.

One of them, a short, stocky man with clammy skin and a tight-fitting uniform, stood at the front of the group. Senator Yuel was next to him, visibly on edge, trying to speak to the guard even as he was on the radio.

Their eyes went to the MEAV as it approached, the senator throwing his hands out in anger.

"We need to hurry," Howard said. "Things are going from bad to worse down there."

The team helped themselves to the armory, stocking up with plenty of ammo. Kilmore took a REX-2025 assault rifle for himself. Age and rank meant nothing when in a hot zone where mutants were rampaging. Additionally, he was a fighter at heart. If he did not have a weapon on hand when on the field, he felt naked.

He joined the team in stepping down the ramp.

"What the hell are you guys doing here?" Senator Yuel shouted.

"Sounds like you people could use a hand," Thomas said.

"There's a minor situation, but we have it under control," Yuel said.

Charity scoffed at the senator's audacity. "What would you consider 'major' then? A nuclear blast?"

Yuel looked at all of them as if they were ghosts. Very quickly, he was starting to get the idea that they knew precisely what was going on.

He looked to the out of shape guard. "Get them out of here."

"I... hold on." The guard lowered the radio's volume. Before he did, Thomas picked up frantic shouting, gunfire, and smashing coming through its receiver.

Yuel pointed at the team. "Have your men get these people off the premises."

The guard, whose tag read 'Clark Hort', stammered. Clearly, he was overwhelmed by the situation, and Yuel's constant demands were only making things more difficult.

Thomas couldn't blame the poor guy, whom he suspected was the night-shift security supervisor, hence Yuel was looking to him to direct the staff while Mylo Noverre and Drey Whiteford were unavailable.

"I... Senator, we're low on manpower and..."

"Shh!" Yuel sliced his hand through the air, clenching his teeth. Clark went silent, realizing he nearly spilled the beans regarding the severity of the situation. He looked at Raptor Pack, not with hostility, but pleading eyes.

General Kilmore went ahead and spoke up. "Look, we already know the situation's out of control. You've got numerous casualties, and by the look of it, you're gonna have a lot more. Unless something is done quickly."

"You don't know jack," Yuel spat.

Kilmore leaned on his professionalism to keep himself in check. A back and forth session throwing insults and testing egos was not going to help anything. Lives were on the line, and the general's only priority was to stop the threat.

"Senator… Stephen, I understand you don't want anything to happen to your son."

Yuel stepped backwards, his jaw hanging open, caught between wanting to publicly deny his relationship with Mylo and demanding how Kilmore knew about them.

"I… there's not… how did…?"

"I get it," Kilmore continued. "He was injured, in constant pain, and disabled. I've seen too many people suffer such a life; many of them having been under my command, both in the Army and in G.O.R.E. Sector. I know you got him here so Dr. Zarek could use the particle to perfect a serum from his formula derived from those deep-underwater fish. But it didn't work. He's a mutant now. There's no reversing the process."

"Worse…" Charity said in an equally sympathetic voice. "He's suffering the primary side effect other than the physical mutation: aggression. Like everything else that has been corrupted by the particle, he has developed an insatiable desire to kill. There's no reasoning with him. There's no rationality. It's an instinct. Sometimes it's supplemented by the need to feed, but even if that was not the case, mutants have a drive to destroy any living thing they come into contact with. I'm sorry."

Senator Yuel's skin brightened. His breathing intensified, worrying those around him that he was about to loose his dinner. His face turned misty and his hands shook.

"I wasn't there for him. All I wanted was to make up for everything. I thought if I healed him with Dr. Zarek's help, it would make it right. I thought the doctor's formula would work; that it would enhance Mylo's healing ability while preventing any negative mutative side effects. I thought it worked."

"I know," Charity said. "But you should've followed Zarek's advice about keeping the test dogs under observation before turning to human trials."

"I know, I know. It's been such a long journey. Mylo's mind was in the slumps. I got impatient, and…" He stopped and looked at the team. In the blink of an eye, he went from remorseful to sternly inquisitive. "Hold on… how do you know about the test dogs? How did you know what Dr. Zarek said to me?"

"Same way we know Mylo's attacking Med/Lab Two," General Kilmore said. He was looking at a tablet Howard had brought out as he spoke. Mylo was rampaging through several guards in the hall. The door slots took a severe hit from his elbow, caving them in, effectively preventing Whiteford from sealing the room.

Gunfire rattled off while the man-beast raged on.

Mylo ripped one of the huge monitoring desks from the floor. Like a caber toss competitor, he launched the huge piece of mechanical equipment across the large room, straight at the doors on the opposite end.

Dr. Zarek and the other scientists barely made it out of the way. The doors on the southeast end of the room bulged outward from the impact, effectively jamming and preventing the staff from escaping that way.

Only one doorway remained.

"Where does that lead to?" Thomas asked.

"It feeds into a few passageways," Howard replied. "Straight ahead is that testing chamber where they performed the test on the dogs."

Thomas looked to Charity. "Mutants are aggressive towards everything, right?"

She nodded. "The only exception being members of a colony, like wasps or the crustaceans in Half-Moon Trench. They retain their normal functions, working together as a single unit. Occasionally, if mutations are siblings, they might work together, like the younger sharks we killed in the trench."

"What are you getting at, Cap?" Renee asked.

"I want to know if a mutant saw *another* mutant, if their intense aggression would lead them to trade blows," Thomas said. He looked at Charity for her opinion.

"Very likely," she said. "We saw that behavior between the hornets and wasps, as well as the crustacean and shark mothers in the trench."

Thomas held his hand towards Clark. "Mind if I borrow your radio?" Clark promptly handed it over. Thomas turned the volume back up and held it to his face. "Drey Whiteford, this is Captain Thomas Rodney from G.O.R.E. Sector."

"Little busy here, Captain!"

"I've noticed. That's why I'm calling through Clark Holt's radio. From what we've observed, Mylo is after Dr. Zarek. Probably because the doctor ordered him to be euthanized after he started mutating. Regardless of the 'why', the carnage won't stop there. Here's what you do: lure Mylo to the testing chamber where the dogs were tested. Release the dogs, then evacuate and lock all doors. Let them be trapped in there and tear each other apart."

"The dogs were euthanized."

"Right. And they were given the same exact treatment as Mylo," Thomas said. "How'd that work out for him?"

There was a moment of radio silence before Whiteford answered.

"Point taken. We're moving."

"Good. Ask the doctor if it's possible to remote operate those holding cells from up here."

A few moments passed, during which Whiteford was getting the answer from the doctor, all while trying to survive the insanity taking place all around him.

"That's affirmative. He just needs to click something on his computer to allow access from the upper security posts."

"Good. Have him relay the information back to Mr. Holt as soon as possible. Then make sure you get the target in that chamber."

"Copy. Hope this works, Captain. I've lost a lot of men."

"At the very least, it'll give you guys an opportunity to get topside," Thomas said.

"Fair enough. I'll take it."

Thomas handed the radio back to Clark, then looked at Renee. "That chinook still in the area?"

"Set down over by the ravine, twelve miles east, just as you and the general insisted."

"Get them over here," he said. "Howard, it seems you might get the chance to give your mountain lions the ultimate field test tonight."

Howard exhaled sharply. "Just what I was afraid of."

CHAPTER 12

"Keep going! Don't stop!"

By now, Drey Whiteford was stating the obvious. Everyone who had survived the clash in Med/Lab Two had no intention of standing toe-to-toe with the mutant.

They ran northwards up Corridor Two-Twelve, with Dr. Zarek in the front of the group. It was not so much that his life was more important than the others, but he was the only surviving scientist who knew the codes by heart.

Behind them, the Mylo creature raced after them.

He showed little sign of fatigue. If anything, the massacre was riling him up all the more.

Gradually, he closed in on the guards running at the back of the group. Their stoicism displayed in battle back in Med/Lab Two was completely gone. All that remained was terror.

"No-no-no-no-no-no!" one of them cried out, feeling the intensifying vibrations from giant footsteps coming up behind him. He knew the monster had set its sights on him, and there was no hope of evading. "Get away from me!"

Mylo granted him his wish—in a sense. Snatching the guard, the man-beast turned on his heel and threw him like a softball. The guard twirled on his way down the steel passageway, bouncing hard off the floor, after which he rag-dolled all the way to Med/Lab Two.

The next guard, sensing a similar fate in his immediate future, decided to go down fighting. He turned to face the beast, aimed high, and landed a few shots to Mylo's brow.

Growling in anger, the mutant hammered a fist directly on top of the guard's head, pancaking him all the way to his boots.

Stepping over the pile of human goo, Mylo charged at the remaining survivors. In addition to Whiteford and Zarek, there were five guards and two scientists still alive.

They were nearing the doors to the testing chamber. Zarek had the door opened and was taking a right to the east doorway. He stopped by the monitoring station, clicked on something a couple of times with the mouse, then joined the rest of the group at the door.

Mylo stepped into the chamber, sporting that ugly smile of his. His shoulders rose and fell, his stamina quickly recharging in the few moments of hiatus.

A mechanical sound caught his ear.

The doors shut behind him and their locking mechanisms engaged. Mylo looked back at them, then at Zarek.

He gave a gravelly chuckle. *What good is shutting doors BEHIND me supposed to do?*

The next mechanical sound came from the center of the room. Mylo's smile shrank a few inches as he took notice of the three glass barriers lifting from their holding cells. Their inner layers were heavily marked, near to the point of the domes losing their structural integrity. Had it not been for the tight quarters of each cell which reduced the amount of leverage for the subjects inside, those domes likely would have been breached.

It did not matter anymore, for they were willfully being freed.

Mylo gave Dr. Zarek a side eye. The procedure for opening those cells required more steps than just a couple of mouse clicks. He granted access to someone else, who did the rest of the work, deliberately unleashing the test subjects. The reason was obvious: they wanted those dogs to kill him.

Three distinct growling sounds reverberated from each shallow dungeon.

The east door opened and the group made their exit all at once, Whiteford shutting it behind them and engaging all locks. The west door was sealed and max-locked as well, effectively sealing Mylo in with his four-legged counterparts.

From the cell on the back left, the first of the trio emerged. What were once furry, innocent paws hammered onto the metallic floor tiles, the tips of half-circle nails creating thin grooves.

The brownish-black fur had fallen off in clumps, revealing red, bumpy flesh underneath with scaly textures. The left eye was bulging outward a little bit, the upper jaw extending six or seven inches ahead of the lower. Those teeth had grown multiple times their original size, as did the tongue, which was now hanging over the lower jaw.

Already, Mylo had a nickname for it.

Odie.

From another cell emerged another former German Shephard. It was roughly the same size as the other, and suffered some of the same bodily deformations regarding skin texture and loss of fur. Its upper and lower jaws had grown more evenly than the one with the big snout. Still, the canine had its own hazard in its mutation, and that was the implosion of one of its eye sockets. It was as though ten-thousand pounds of pressure came down on the side of its face, collapsing part of its skull. The other eye was red, save for the black pupil, and fixed on the humanoid mutant across the chamber.

True to his old marine sense of humor, Mylo thought up a nickname.

Cyclops.

The third mutant canine jumped out of its cell. Right away, Mylo noticed how its lips were completely gone, leaving dark red gums and white teeth protruding from them.

Its left shoulder was hunched, with spines protruding in a manner similar to those from Mylo's elbows and shoulders.

But the most distinct feature came in the form of its nails. During the mutation process, its toes on its two front feet appeared to have fused together to form something similar to a hoof. From the center of that hoof was the result of its many nails having fused together, forming a three-foot-long razor-sharp scythe which appeared sharp enough to dice a human in half.

Mylo chuckled at that thought. Fortunately for him, he was no longer human.

This time, he relied on innocent memories from Saturday morning movie viewings to forge the beast's nickname.

Gigan.

The three canines howled demented sounds at their bipedal challenger.

Mylo leaned forward and threw his hands to the side, bellowing his reply. Following his monstrous sound came a thunderous challenge.

"Bring it!"

Cyclops was first to make a move. Bounding through the air with jaws wide open, he closed in on Mylo.

A heavy backhanded swipe cut the dog's attack short, knocking it to the west side of the room. Cyclops hit the ground and rolled over. He righted himself, shaking his head to clear his senses.

Odie was next to make a move. His approach was to gallop at the humanoid like a racehorse, his tongue flapping over the corner of his mouth.

Mylo broke into a sprint, meeting the canine head-on. He thrust one of his elbows out, driving those spines into the soft flesh of Odie's right cheek. The dog howled and pulled his face free.

A right hook to that oversized snout put Odie into a tailspin. Mylo landed a kick against the scaly flesh of his hind quarters, putting the dog skidding over the floor.

The third member of the trio proved much more difficult to handle. Gigan came at Mylo at full speed. Knowing what its greatest advantage was, the deformed dog reared on its back legs after coming within a few feet of the humanoid. Still driven forward by its momentum, it thrust those front feet and their talons forward.

Mylo's grin vanished in a nanosecond. He doubled over, hands clutching those legs, but not in time to prevent those talons from plunging eight inches into both sides of his ribcage.

Drooling thick globs of saliva, the dog looked him right in the eye, knowing exactly what it was doing as it put all of its power into driving those so-called paws deeper.

Its two companions righted themselves and began moving in on their common foe, ready to get a taste.

Mylo did not break eye contact with Gigan. The dog clearly thought it had this fight won.

"Bad dog!"

He thrust his hands forward, removing those talons from his body, then shoved the dog back. Gigan made another lunge, claws coming for Mylo's throat.

An uppercut caught the dog on its chin, ejecting one of its teeth from its gums. Gigan reeled backwards, its four limbs slashing the air in anger.

The other two closed in, securing sharp holds on his left forearm and right leg. Mylo teetered left and right, the two opponents pulling in different directions. The aching in his midsection was not helping matters.

Cyclops, holding on to his leg, yanked backward.

Mylo corkscrewed to the right and fell on his back, the momentum inadvertently pulling Odie on top of him. The mutant dog maintained his grasp on his left arm, driving those teeth two inches deep on both sides, the tongue flapping about.

He sneered, feeling Cyclops' teeth tearing his calf and shin as it attempted to pull the leg off.

In the corner of his eye, he saw Gigan righting himself, ready to get back into the fray.

Mylo pulled his left arm high, bringing Odie's face closer to his. It was at this moment that he demonstrated the severity of *his* bite.

Odie spasmed from the intense pain of Mylo driving his own teeth. The humanoid did not go for an arm, shoulder, or even the face—he went for the throat.

Its jaws released, but it did not separate, for Mylo maintained his vicious grip. With every passing moment, he applied additional pressure to his bite, tasting the blood of his panicking foe.

Odie was flailing now, eyes wide, tongue extended directly outward.

Mylo's teeth intertwined, severing a raw chunk of the dog-mutant's throat. It reeled backward, a red fountain jetting from its jugular.

Landing on its back, it pedaled its legs, its sides rising and falling rapidly as its lungs tried to take in fresh oxygen.

Spitting out the meat, Mylo rolled to his knees, enduring the additional tearing of flesh on his leg while giving himself better leverage to engage Cyclops. The dog, sensing the turning of the tide, released Mylo's bleeding leg. It launched off its back legs in an effort to tackle the humanoid on his back.

Mylo sidestepped and hit the dog in the face with a haymaker. The canine, baring teeth, faceplanted on the floor. Right away, it pushed itself upright and turned around to resume the fight. Mylo was right in its face, ready with a flurry of devastating punches.

Cyclops' head whipped left and right, his teeth cracking, his skull gradually deforming from crushing impacts capable of breaking through steel.

A kick to one of its front legs dropped the grotesque canine to its chest. It scowled in anger and pain, its leg broken in two places.

Clicking and scraping sounds from his seven o'clock alerted Mylo to Gigan's assault. The dog was coming in hot, intent on driving those talons through his back.

Grabbing Cyclops by the neck, Mylo rotated one-hundred-and-twenty degrees, putting the injured mutant between himself and Gigan's talons. The dog had risen on its back legs again, thrusting its bone blades forward.

Cyclops convulsed, his one eye bursting to jelly. Its companion's huge claw punched deep through the eye socket, inadvertently piercing the brain. The no-eyed canine went limp, permanently out of the fight.

Mylo threw a kick, knocking Gigan backward. He followed up the attack by grabbing the dog by its ears, ramming his knee into its face, then dragging it in a circle. At the end of the rotation, Gigan was launched across the room, faceplanting against the control monitor.

Mylo took a breath, confirming that Cyclops was dead.

Odie was still breathing, though sporadically, losing blood by the gallon.

In this moment, Mylo looked down at himself to inspect his own injuries. The findings returned that ugly smile to his face, for Dr. Zarek's formula had proven to be more successful than he originally thought.

The wounds were sealed, the bleeding stopped.

In addition to enhanced size and strength, he was given the gift of rapid regeneration.

The discovery proved to be a warning. If the serum had given him the capability of healing severe injuries within a minute or two, it was safe to assume the dogs had the same advantage. Judging by Cyclops' stiff corpse, they were not immortal. Should the brain be destroyed, gone would be the gift of regeneration.

Realizing this fact, Mylo realized he needed to act fast to keep Odie out of the fight.

Doing so was simple. And, to his demented mind, fun.

He leapt onto the canine and pummeled its skull with his fists.

BAM! BAM! BAM! BAM! BAM!

Again and again, he hammered Odie's head. The skull was tough, but unable to withstand so many concentrated hits in such quick succession. After thirty seconds, its head was flattened, the brain crushed, its life ended.

Mylo stood up, hands still clenched into fists, his soul exhilarated by what he had just accomplished.

That joy turned reverted back to tension as Gigan closed in for another attack. This time, he went low, wrapping his jaws around Mylo's knee. Yanking backwards, he twisted into a death roll, identical to a crocodile's signature move.

Mylo corkscrewed and hit the floor, his vision nothing but a haze of spinning metal walls.

He leaned forward and grunted, feeling one of those claws slash across his stomach.

This dog didn't even act like a dog. Cyclops and Odie, though horribly deformed and incredibly violent, at least relied on the same general tactics in fighting as their uncontaminated counterparts did.

But Gigan was a completely different animal entirely. He fought like an alien monster from space— precisely like the character he was named after.

However, there was one common trend in every film he appeared in. In spite of his ruthless fighting abilities, he was always defeated in the end.

Mylo chose to stay true to that trend.

The canine slashed again, severely lacerating his chest.

Mylo, groaning in pain, brought his knee up and planted his heel against the dog's chest. Kicking outward, he launched Gigan back several meters.

Bleeding from his many wounds, he pushed himself to his feet. They would heal, so long as his opponent did not land a fatal blow.

The dog stood on its four legs and faced the humanoid, maintaining its constant snarl. It inhaled repeatedly, charging its veins for another go. The claws tapped the floor, grooving the metal tiles with ease.

Mylo remained in place, anticipating the quadrupedal mutant's next move. It began to quiver, the moment of attack almost arrived.

Its plan was foiled, as Mylo charged first.

After just four steps, he jumped high, grabbing one of the glass domes that hovered over a cell. Detaching it from its cable, he came down, holding the massive bell-shaped object over his head.

With every ounce of energy, he slammed it down on Gigan's head. The dog was flattened against the floor, resembling a starfish with its limbs sprawled in all directions. Glass shattered, tearing its flesh in multiple locations.

Mylo did not waste time. The canine was stunned, but would quickly return to the fight unless decisive action was taken.

Looking at several enormous glass shards, shaped like perfect daggers, he decided to use the dog's own tactic to win the day. Unlike Gigan, Mylo had a conscious understanding of how to defeat his foe.

He grabbed the dog by the face and pulled up, forcing its mouth open. Its wits quickly started to return, and it attempted to bite.

Mylo, needing the dog to remain still, clasped its head with both hands, and gave a sharp twist.

CRACK!

The dog went limp, its neck broken.

As Mylo expected, it was still alive. It was breathing, the hind legs twitching. Soon, the regenerative process would repair the spinal injury. As long as the brain remained intact, the creature would be up and running, ready to continue the fight.

He looked at the glass shards and gave more thought to driving one of them through the roof of its mouth and into the brain.

Nah.

He went with something more brutal.

Planting his foot on the dog's shoulder, he grabbed its head and pulled straight up.

Flesh and bone stretched, then split. Blood poured in thick currents, the head detaching from the broken neck.

Mylo held the severed head in front of his face, looking his dead foe in the eyes in search of any sign of life. The face was still as ice, the eyes pale, the skin under the remaining fur losing color.

He waited patiently, holding the head like a ghastly hand puppet. There was no regeneration, no movement, no life.

It was here that Mylo learned the brain itself did not need to be destroyed. Detaching it from the spinal column was enough to do the trick. A severed head would not regenerate an entire body. It still needed the advantage of blood flow and a beating heart. Even if the heart was damaged, it would regenerate quickly enough to resume its duties.

The key to his longevity was the brain.

He tossed the dog's head over his shoulder. "Let's not lose our heads."

Now that the fight was over, it was time to get back to his original task. Zarek and the others had retreated through the east doors.

It took several hits and a bit of patience, but Mylo got through them. He emerged on the other side and looked at the elevator doors. Common sense dictated that his intended victims went to the surface.

Alarms were blaring throughout the entire underground facility. An evacuation was being ordered.

Good. Bring them all to the surface. It'll be like fish in a barrel.

With that in mind, he punched his way through one of the elevator doors, widening it enough to get himself into the shaft.

Grabbing anything he could, he began his climb to the surface.

CHAPTER 13

"Elevator's up. We're coming out."

Clark Holt gave a sigh of relief after receiving Drey Whiteford's update. "Copy that. Team Seven, you there?"

"Copy that," the team leader replied. *"We've got eyes on the survivors. We're bringing them out now."*

Outside the station, a downdraft was kicking up dust into the night air. The chinook set down on the parking lot and immediately lowered its cargo hold. Dozens of security personnel stood dumbfounded, watching the three quadrupedal machines step outside.

They formed a single row, facing their creator and awaited instructions. Their shoulder-mounted turrets were armed and ready to go, their 'eyes' glowing bright green in the dark of night.

Furthering the intrigue of everyone watching, they responded to *verbal* commands given by Thomas Rodney.

"Number One, cover the south lot. Number Two, cover the loading bay. Number Three, remain here."

One and Two galloped out of sight, the layout of the facility having been downloaded into their computer system.

Clark Holt stared blankly, his eyebrows stretched high.

"Um... nice pets you have there."

"Thanks. They're expensive," Howard remarked.

The main doors opened and out came the few survivors of Mylo's rampage. Medical crew quickly assessed the science staff. Whiteford, his face discolored with bumps, bruises, and oily smears, immediately went to General Kilmore, paying no mind to Senator Yuel and the facility administration, who had arrived just a few minutes ago. He was exhausted, physically and mentally, and had no desire to speak with people who had no idea how to contain the situation.

"General. Raptor Pack." He gave the welcome visitors a nod of appreciation, taking notice of the MEAV M2 behind them. "Engine trouble, huh?"

Renee shrugged nonchalantly. "What can I say? Machines can be stubborn."

Whiteford was looking at the mountain lion robot as she said that. "Not too stubborn, I hope."

Thomas looked past him at the main entrance. "How many men do you have inside?"

Whiteford looked to Clark for an answer to that. "We still have people in there, aside from Team Seven?"

"Yes, but nobody in the sublevels," Clark answered. "I lost track of the target. The cameras went out while he was fighting the dogs. We can't get them back."

Howard, unable to access the mosquito drones through his tablet, hurried to his desk inside *Firebird-Two*. The feed came through just in time for them to witness Mylo taking on the last surviving German Shepherd.

He winced, seeing the canine lose its head in gruesome fashion. "Well, at least they slowed him down."

The mutated Mylo Noverre proceeded to smash through one of the doorways. He took a look at the elevators. For a few moments, he stood there.

Howard could practically read his thoughts.

"He's strategizing."

"Where is he?" Thomas called to him.

Howard swallowed, witnessing the creature rip through the elevator doors and squeeze his way into the shaft.

The mosquito drone followed Mylo inside, angling the camera upward, allowing the engineer to bear witness to the mutant's rapid ascent to the surface levels.

"He's coming up the elevator shaft!"

His words were punctuated by a thundering *SMASH* from within the facility. Tremors shook the ground. Gunshots popped off from the corridors. Gradually, those intense vibrations were overshadowed by the screams of horrified men as they were being torn apart one after another.

General Kilmore turned to the flight crew near the chinook. "Get everybody on board! We're evacuating." He turned to Yuel. "Senator, get aboard now."

Yuel did not hear a word he said.

Like a granite figure, he stared blankly at the station, hypnotized by the horrible sounds coming from inside.

They were coming from one of the corridors on the east side. Little by little, those sounds moved south, intensifying exponentially until the beast came through the south wall.

Pieces of steel, concrete, and insulation flew from the breach, peppering nearby vehicles.

Mylo stepped into the open, holding a guard in each hand. He stood straight, having used his shoulder to plow through the exterior wall, and admired his audience before giving them a show with his two struggling captives.

He smacked the two men together and tossed them over his shoulders, snarling at the dozens of troops in front of him.

Senator Yuel collapsed to his knees, beholding the consequences of his ambition. The efforts to help Mylo had turned him into something he was never supposed to be. Mylo was an honorable marine and a decent human. It was all he had left to hold on to. Instead of taking away his misery, Yuel took away his honor. All that remained was the beast, and the carnage left in its wake.

Mylo turned to a group of soldiers, who shot him with their useless rifles. He bent his knees and sprung himself off the ground, traveling the twenty feet of distance. He came down in the middle of the group, crushing two of them under his heels.

Thrusting his elbow to the side, he speared another one through the chest. With that same arm, he threw a haymaker, pulverizing another guard and sending his body skidding across the ground for several yards.

Rotating to his right, Mylo laid eyes on Dr. Zarek. He was in the glow of the spotlights, moving with the other staff to the chinook.

He followed the doctor with his eyes, momentarily losing visual as Zarek passed behind the MEAV M2.

Mylo perked up, taking notice of the advanced aircraft and the monster hunters who had ridden on it. They stood a few yards from its starboard thruster, watching him. They held guns he had never seen before. He had heard rumors of how the organization invented all sorts of new things, whether it was for exploration or extermination. Sure enough, it was true.

None of that unnerved the giant; especially not after what he had gone through in the animal testing chamber. He was already back to tiptop shape, with nothing but thin, faint scars from where he had been bitten and slashed.

"Monster hunters!" he roared.

Renee gulped. The thing sounded like a true demon lifted straight from Satan's fiery kingdom. Looked like one too.

"Not used to having them *talk* to us," she muttered.

"Yeah…" An equally unnerved Howard Tate replied.

Archer stepped in front of the group, more than happy to engage the mutant. "Just say the word, Cap."

Mylo grunted and winded up a fist, taunting Raptor Pack.

"One thing first." Thomas pulled his transmitter from his pocket. "Alright, Archer. Light him up."

Mylo sniggered, anticipating a wave of futile rifle fire.

To his shock, all the soldier sent from the barrel of his gun was a thin line of green light.

The beast looked at the tiny speck on his chest. Right away, he recognized the technology.

He was being lased.

He looked to the air, expecting to see a Lockheed AC-130 laying down air support. But the sky was clear.

"Go get him, boys," Thomas said.

Mechanical legs battered the ground behind Mylo. The beast turned around, his red eyes bulging as one of the mountain lions charged in.

Strangely enough, the sight of four-legged robots running at him was far more bizarre than standing face-to-face with three mutant dogs.

There were two robots, both as large as the dogs he had recently fought. Muzzle flashes sparked from their backs.

Mylo reeled backward, having literally absorbed over thirty forty-five-caliber rounds. They entered his chest at terminal velocity; their combined stopping power, along with the pain from the internal damage they caused, putting the mutant on the ground.

A familiar taste of blood filled Mylo's mouth.

He spat, grimacing from feeling his organs literally being split open.

Following his fall, the entire area went silent. The two robots moved in on him with caution, angling their gun muzzles to his head.

Near the MEAV, Thomas and his crew watched in dreaded anticipation.

"Did we get him?" Renee asked.

Thomas shook his head. Something wasn't right.

"Finish him off," he ordered the machines.

Mylo's strained face turned to one of mischief. In one fluid motion, he rolled to his hands and knees, backhanding one of the robots before it could unload on him.

The machine skidded across the ground, hitting the second robot and throwing off its aim.

Mylo took a moment to face the members of Raptor Pack, making sure his torso could be seen in the outside lights. The holes in his flesh closed before their very eyes.

"Whoa..." Renee gasped. "This might be a little harder than we thought."

Mylo turned around and lunged at the machines.

Number Two was struck from behind, its head driven into the concrete. Grabbing ahold of its neck, Mylo lifted the machine until it was standing on its hind legs—right as Number One let loose another barrage of gunfire.

Sparks flew as bullets riddled Number Two's underside. Its companion ceased fire, detecting the friendly between it and the target.

Maintaining his grasp, Mylo began twisting the neck. Oil leaked and sparks flashed, while gears protested as the head was twisted beyond their limits.

Just as he had done with the third mutant dog, Mylo tore the head off the mountain lion drone. The body fell on its side, the legs twitching in the same manner as a freshly killed corpse.

Howard closed his eyes.

There goes another invention.

Number One hit the beast with a burst of gunfire, driving him back. Running at full speed, it thrust its front legs, clubbing Mylo across the face. His jaw detached, hanging only by loose flesh. More blows struck his ribcage and chest, cracking bone and inflicting great pain.

Number Three joined in, tearing into Mylo's abdomen with a burst of ammunition.

The mutant dropped to one knee, his jaw swaying back and forth, the eyes wide, conveying distress as well as agony. Even with the advantage of his healing factor, Mylo was undoubtedly worried about the outcome of this fight.

The increased strength of their heavy machine-guns in comparison to the soldiers' rifles made much of the difference. Unlike the dogs, these machines had the advantage of ranged attacks.

His feeling of invincibility was dwindling. If he was injured faster than he could regenerate, then it would do him no good. He'd still be a goner. The only difference was his death would be more humiliating, for he had gone into a fight with a supreme advantage and still was bested.

The feeling was hammered in—quite literally—as one of the robots struck him on the brow with their feet.

Flat on his back, his head throbbing, his blood spilling onto the dirt and concrete, Mylo recognized his limitations. His killing spree in the lower levels had given him an inflated sense of dauntlessness. Only now did he truly realize his reign of terror could be stopped.

But the desire to kill remained. Not only did it remain, but it was *enhanced.*

Thus, he formed a new strategy. Winning did not only come by winning every single physical clash, but rather from outsmarting the enemy and attacking from an angle they did not anticipate. If they had greater numbers and firepower, sometimes it was necessary to cause a distraction by attacking a completely different target.

As he lay on his back, he squinted at the lights shining down on him.

Power.

The Granger Valley Research Facility had its very own power source, courtesy of the nuclear plant a half mile northwest. Technically, it also provided power to the towns thirty miles away. It was just something to appease the public, but its true purpose was to keep Granger online twenty-four-seven.

Nuclear power. It was the cleanest energy mankind had discovered, so long as it was kept under control.

His grimace turned into a smile.

He knew exactly how to get there and where to strike.

Mylo had his alternate strategy. The present clash with the weapons of G.O.R.E. Sector may have been too much for him to handle, but the war was his for the win. A breach of that reactor core and death would befall upon everyone in a thousand square miles.

All the while, his gift of regeneration would prevent him from suffering the woes of radiation poisoning.

First, he needed to get there.

Mylo rolled to his right, dodging a hammering strike from one of the machines. Its foot came down where his head had been, cracking the pavement. Rolling to his knees, he grabbed the mechanical creature by the wrist, then spun in a counterclockwise motion.

The robot was lifted off the ground, its hind legs pedaling the air. Mylo let go, letting the machine fly straight into the other one. Both robots bounced head over feet across the ground, granting him the opportunity to retreat into the station.

"Look out!" Thomas yelled.

Raptor Pack and the security guards standing with them dispersed, clearing the path for the skidding robots. Metal screeched, the concrete marking their perfect silver finish.

Pushing with their legs, the mountain lions righted themselves and turned around, ready to resume the fight. Their guns rotated in search of a target that had abruptly disappeared.

The team regrouped.

"Everyone alright?" Thomas said.

"Except for one of my machines," Howard said in a bitter voice. "They almost had him, too."

"Where is he?" Charity asked.

Whiteford used his radio to connect with some men over by the east end of the complex. "Anyone down there have a visual?"

"Negative. He disappeared back into the station."

Thomas used his communicator to instruct the mountain lions. "Enter breach. Pursue target."

Like hunting dogs, they raced through the gaping hole in the building. Their visual feeds came through on Howard's tablet.

Thomas watched the droids move through a long line of devastation. Offices, conference rooms, and coffee areas had been ravaged. The brute had tore through the walls, leaving pieces of drywall spread across the floor with battered furniture.

The machines followed the path all the way to the elevator shafts. Microphones picked up vibrations from below, confirming Mylo had returned to the sublevels.

"He's underground again," Howard said.

"Nice work, Doctor," Kilmore said. "Looks like your toys proved a little too much for him after all. At the very least, they're giving us an opportunity to evacuate everyone out of this place. On that note…"

The general stepped away to make some phone calls, leaving his team to develop a new course of action.

"Where's he going?" Thomas asked Howard. "Do we have a visual?"

"I've got my bugs heading in that direction," Howard said. "I've got nothing from the station's functioning cameras so far."

"Captain," Ray Archer spoke up. The captain turned to face him, knowing that if Archer had something to say, it was important. "We might have to send those bots into the tunnels after that thing. More importantly, replace their guns with rocket or grenade launchers. Hit it with something it cannot walk away from."

Renee chuckled. "No need for that. Just lure him back up here after the area is evacuated. Once he's in the open, I can hit him with a bunch of missiles. His *Wolverine* healing abilities won't mean shit if I vaporize his ass."

"We can kill him that way, right?" Whiteford asked.

"I imagine so," Charity said. "That's why he retreated. Also, the dogs were exposed to the same formula, and they're dead as a doornail. He's obviously not invincible."

"Good to know," Thomas said. "Renee, go ahead and take to the sky. We'll figure out a way to flush him out. Howard, go in there with her. You need your little gaming system to control your drones anyway."

Howard made a face. "I wouldn't put it so artlessly, but yes."

He ran with Renee into *Firebird-Two*.

"There is one other thing to consider," Kilmore chimed in, having completed one of his calls. "Unlike most other targets, which rely mainly on instinct, we're dealing with a marine. A combat veteran. Though he's screwed up in the head as well as his body, he's not dumb. He clearly understands how to plan his attacks, and he appears to know his limits."

Thomas thought for a moment, taking that information into account.

"He's not just going down there to retreat. He's got something in mind. Whatever it is, it's not good."

"I've got a visual!" Howard shouted from his desk. "He's heading north. No... correction... northwest."

"Sublevel Two again?" Thomas asked.

"Negative... Sublevel One," Howard replied. "Moving fast, too. My drones can't keep up with him. But I'd say he's moving with intent."

"Could be readying himself to attack from the west side of the station," Archer suggested.

Thomas looked to Whiteford. "Is there anything in Sublevel-One that would interest him?"

The security commander shook his head. "Nothing but labs down there. Unless he figured out some crazy combination of lab chemicals to create a toxic cloud, there's nothing of use for him down there..."

He suddenly went quiet, having been stricken by a terrible realization after hearing that speculation spoken out loud.

The hairs on the back of Thomas' neck stood on end. He thought about the layout of the complex Howard had mapped out during their initial sweep.

"Oh, crap! The underground tunnel to the power plant."

Charity's face turned red. "He's gonna try and breach their reactor cores and create a meltdown."

"There'll be a cloud of radioactive gas spewed into the atmosphere," Thomas said. "If we don't all die on the spot, we'll be dead by cancer in a few years at the latest."

"Not just us," Charity said. "This desert will not protect the nearest populated areas. Not if we're unable to contain the meltdowns. And we won't be able to if Mylo remains in the area."

"He'd attack any response team. We wouldn't be able to use appropriate tactics against him; not if he's near the reactor cores. Any explosion would only make the problem worse." Thomas inhaled through his nostrils, suppressing the burst of anxiety which threatened to hinder his decision-making process.

Firebird-Two was lifting off.

Thomas clicked his radio transmitter. "Lieutenant?"

"Oh, don't tell me you need me to come back down already."

"Nope, you have a new target; one that will require every missile and bomb you have at your disposal."

"Oh?"

"Move northwest. There's an underground tunnel. The mutation is going to use it to reach the nuclear plant. You understand what I'm saying?"

"Crystal clear, Captain." Renee's voice was void of her usual swagger. *"I'll cut him off."*

"I'll get you some surface markers to identify precise targeting areas, so you know where to strike," Thomas said.

"No need," Howard said. *"I have the schematic uploaded from our initial sweep. We already know exactly where to strike."*

"Excellent. Get it done," Thomas said.

Firebird-Two zipped overhead, vanishing over the structure, the blue glow of its thrusters illuminating the black sky.

"All units, clear the northwest perimeter immediately," Whiteford warned his personnel through the radio. "I repeat, clear the area. This second. This is an emergency."

***

Mylo started to laugh. He was more than halfway through Sublevel-One when all of the containment doors sealed shut. Many of them were made from an inch-thick slab of steel, compared to the much larger containment barriers downstairs. For any human, these doors were more than sufficient to prevent passage. But for him, they were a minor inconvenience.

At each juncture, he left a trail of devastation in his wake.

After a few short minutes, he had passed through Genetics and into the outer corridors. As he expected, the barrier to the northwest tunnel was shut.

It was obvious this was the work of those upstairs. Whiteford, at the instruction of G.O.R.E. Sector, had sealed every passageway. It was either a pitiful attempt to keep him locked in, or they were aware of where he was going. Either way, it was a laughable effort.

He was fully healed now, with nothing more than mild soreness in his jaw leftover from the skirmish with the robots. Raptor Pack did well with their weapons development.

Not good enough.

In a single strike, he breached the barrier leading into the northwest tunnel. Laying waste to the door, he looked into the darkness straight ahead. It was a straight half-mile-long sprint to his objective.

There, the fun would *really* begin.

He imagined the frenzied efforts of the United States government in attempting to contain the upcoming disaster. Every action would be thwarted by him, forcing them to send more people in. All the while, he would resist the radiation long enough to destroy any response team and allow the cloud of poison to flood the atmosphere.

With that thought in mind, he charged into the tunnel. Surrounded by darkness, he quickened his speed, the evil deed calling to him like a seductive voice.

BOOM!

The tunnel shook.

Mylo stopped, his newfound enthusiasm making way for concern. He knew the sound of an explosion when he heard it.

BOOM!

BOOM!

BOOM!

The ceiling opened and the earth rained down.

Concrete and dirt struck the mutant's brow, driving him to the floor. All the while, the explosions resumed.

Between the blasts was the sound of many tons of earth and tunnels caving in on Mylo's path. Whoever did the shooting knew exactly where to strike. Considering the artillery being used, it had to have been that fancy aircraft used by G.O.R.E. Sector.

The beast pulled himself clear of the rubble, then stood back up.

Growling, he glared at the jampacked mountain of blockage in his path. It was practically invisible in the darkness, but there nonetheless.

Giant fists clenched. Those people on the surface knew his intentions—they *knew* he was headed for the nuclear plant.

Smart bastards.

Even with his strength, it would take a significant amount of time to dig through the dirt and concrete in his path. In that time, Raptor Pack could strike. Moving across the surface was equally suicidal. He would be out in the open, vulnerable to the use of explosives. And there was no doubt in his demented mind they planned on upping the ante.

Mylo stomped his foot, cracking the small roadway underneath him. His plan was perfect. It would have been the ultimate defeat for his new enemies. Not only would they die, but they would meet their ends knowing hundreds of thousands, if not millions, were doomed. It would be a catastrophe for the history books; one that would have brought the country to its knees.

He was so close.

So close.

There was no worse feeling than having success in the palm of your hand, only to have it stripped away at the last second.

Mylo rolled his jaw. His internal temper tantrum was over. It was time to come up with a new strategy.

The odds were against him. Sooner or later, there would be more military forces sent down here to smoke him out. They would be using more than M1 Carbines. Armor-piercing rounds, grenades, and even rockets were bound to be used. Sure, Mylo would succeed in killing several men in the process, but in the end, even his healing ability would not protect him.

In addition, there was no underground method of escape. Ultimately, it would take a small army of mutants to overcome the wrath that was heading his way.

An army...

Mylo closed his eyes. A warm feeling rushed over him.

An army was not out of the question. Nor was his desire for large-scale disaster. It would not come from radioactive waste, but the spawning of tens, if not hundreds of mutants, just like him, rampaging across the countryside.

His own enemies would become his pawns. The cargo they had delivered directly to him would be the catalyst.

X41.

Mylo reversed direction and reentered the facility. Utilizing his memory of the layout, he made his way to Sublevel-Three.

CHAPTER 14

"There! I just got a visual. It worked, Captain. We cut him off."

"Excellent news, Howard. Where's he headed now?"

"Stand by..."

Thomas made eye contact with Archer. Without needing a word spoken to him, the sergeant gathered Whiteford and several of his guards and set up a firing line. Two National Guard choppers had arrived and deployed a small platoon of troops. In addition, the two MEAV M1s had successfully double-backed to the site. Lieutenant Belanger led two units of G.O.R.E. Sector troops into the perimeter.

In addition to the increased manpower, the lieutenant gave Archer a nice little gift in the form of an M136 AT4.

Receiving the weapon produced a rare sparkle in the sniper's eye.

Thomas knew exactly what he thought: *We're keeping a few of these in the MEAV from now on.*

Frankly, Thomas agreed with the sentiment.

"Everyone, keep your eyes open," General Kilmore announced. "We've got him trapped down there. He's probably aware the situation is not going in his favor. But, no matter how drastically the scales tip, he's not going to surrender."

"If he gets angry enough, he'll attempt another blitz," Thomas said. "Even these mutations can get desperate when they feel they're backed into a corner."

The combination of National Guard, G.O.R.E. Sector, and Granger Valley security personnel waited in tense silence. Belanger's group watched the east part of the facility where the loading bay was located. Whiteford guarded west with some of his own men and guardsmen.

Any minute now, that beast could show its ugly face.

One minute turned into two.

Then three.

During that time, Thomas started noticing some eyes glancing in his direction.

Clearing his throat, he pressed his radio transmitter. "Uh, Howard?"

"Yeah?"

"Any update? We're kinda just, you know… standing around, waiting for the monster to attack. Would like to know if it's gonna start any time soon."

"Stand by."

The captain mumbled, "I've *been* standing by."

A fourth minute went by.

"Got him! He was in a section of Sublevel-Two where the grid went down during the attack. It appears he's trying to access the freight elevator shaft. I haven't been able to get a layout of the third sublevel. Not sure what he's up to."

The reprieve Thomas felt from averting a nuclear catastrophe was yanked away, and a new sense of trepidation took hold of him.

Perhaps Mylo's crusade for mass genocide was not over yet.

"I think I know." He moved over to where Whiteford was positioned. "He's trying to get into the third sublevel. Is that where you guys were storing X41?"

"That's correct," Whiteford replied. "Wait, you think Mylo's going after it?"

"He obviously thought he was going to cause problems with the nuclear reactor. That mutagen has really turned the poor guy into a freakish psychopath. If he can't cause a meltdown, why not use the meteorite? Release its particles? Contaminate *all* of us?"

Whiteford clenched his teeth while he wrapped his mind around the possibility presented to him.

"Frankly, I'm out of my element here, Captain. I've only encountered one mutant, and it was a rat in a controlled setting, similar to the chamber where they had the dogs."

"Start with this then," Thomas said. "Where is the meteorite being held down there? And how secure is it?"

"It's in a cell titled Sixth Chamber. The meteorite itself is contained in a spherical shell. Literally, a steel casing has been fitted around the rock. The case has plenty of advanced gadgets to allow Dr. Zarek to retrieve samples without risking an uncontrolled breach of the meteorite. The shell is pretty tough. But…"

Thomas was able to complete his thought. "Like all things, it can be taken apart."

"Exactly."

"And Mylo knows how to do it."

"It'll take him a while," Charity joined in. "If he plans to do what you suspect, he can't risk breaching the rock down there. He'll need to handle the shell delicately. Those meteorites are like grenades; they're made to burst upon impact. Some just so happened to be duds, so to speak. My point is: Mylo knows he'll have to be careful freeing the meteorite, and equally as careful getting it up here."

"Mark my words, he's capable of doing it," Whiteford said.

"That I believe," Thomas said. He rested the barrel of his rifle on his shoulder and began brainstorming a new plan. "We're gonna have to go down there."

"Down *there?*" Whiteford's words came out as a wheeze. "I lost God-knows how many men in just a few minutes, Captain. I'm not sure engaging Mylo in such tight quarters is a good idea. It would play right into his hands."

"So would letting him bring the fight to us," Thomas said. "Unless we'd rather transform into something that looks just like him."

Charity stuck her tongue out.

"No thanks."

"You'd be limited in how you'd be able to engage him," Whiteford said. "There's all sorts of unstable elements down there. You can't shoot bazookas, toss grenades, and spray bullets crazily. That's why the area is sealed down as tight as it is. And don't forget, his skin is pretty damn tough, so infantry weapons, including yours, are probably not going to do much. You'd need a chain gun. And even then, good luck not hitting X41 and contaminating yourselves. If you guys mutate into *Hulk* things, what do you think you're gonna do? You'll come straight up here and fight us."

Thomas made eye contact with Charity. "Pressure's on, isn't it?"

She shrugged. "When isn't it?"

"Right?" Thomas bit his lip, trying to think of a quick solution. "We need to strip him of his regenerative capabilities."

Charity laughed. "Wow, why didn't I think of that? Just go down there, take his healing factor away, and shoot him to death. Just like that."

"Cute," Thomas remarked. "But no, I was thinking something more on the line of reversing the process. Maybe using Zarek's formula?"

Charity put a hand on her head. The pressure was really on tonight.

"It's *possible*. But I'd have to get a look at his work. And, frankly, I'm not sure if I can synthesize something fast enough."

"What if I came with you and lent a hand?"

The team looked to the south, surprised to see Dr. Zarek walking up to them. A few steps behind him was Senator Yuel. His collar was loosened and his tie was fully removed, the guy looking sickly.

"You think it's reversible?" Thomas asked the doctor.

"If your specialist can help me isolate a few markers in the original formula, we might be able to alter his mutation," Zarek said.

"Alter?" Thomas wasn't sure he liked the use of that word. "So, either it'll make him weaker, or it might make him stronger. Am I close?"

Zarek exhaled sharply, hating to acknowledge that possibility.

"Pretty much."

"What are the odds of the bad result happening?" Thomas said.

Zarek did the math in his head. "Small chance?"

Thomas sensed the question mark in that answer.

"Ninety-ten? Eighty-twenty?"

Zarek scratched the back of his head. "Sixty-forty, probably."

Thomas turned around. "That's not *small*, Doc!"

"You have a better idea?" Zarek said.

"Yeah," Thomas said. "Blow the whole place up."

"And if he doesn't die?" General Kilmore asked. "If he were to survive a full detonation, we'd never find him. Give it time, he'd tunnel out of here and go on a rampage somewhere else."

Thomas felt the need to sit down. He had to make a decision. Should the plan not work, they could potentially be up against a Mylo Noverre that was twice as powerful. Should his mutation advance in his favor, he could grow strong enough to withstand explosives.

On the other hand, they were short on viable options.

"How would we get the serum into him?" he asked. "Gas him?"

"It wouldn't work outside of a holding cell," Zarek said. "We'd have to inject him."

"Oh, right." Thomas chuckled. This was getting better and better. "I'm sure we can get a needle in him, no problem."

"We can use tranquilizer darts loaded with the serum," Zarek said. "We have them on hand for some of our animal test subjects. They pack a good punch, since we anticipated some mutated subjects having thick skin." He ran his hand over the back of his head again, his expression uncomfortable. "Though, not as tough as Mylo's."

"What if we wounded him?" Charity said. "Shoot him with a fifty-caliber round from a Pterosaur rifle. That'll get through. Then, before the wound heels, hit him through the bullet hole with the dart."

Zarek stared dumbly. "I mean, *technically* that's doable. But, come on, there's nobody in the world who could pull off that shot?" He chuckled nervously, gradually getting quieter as he noticed everyone turning their eyes to Archer.

The sniper gave his usual thumbs up.

Yep. I can do it.

Thomas groaned. "Looks like we're committed. Let's get this over with because, you know our beer ritual at the end of every mission? I'm needing it now."

"Same here," Charity said.

The captain lifted the verbal control device from his pocket. "Number One, Number Three, deactivate turrets. Prep for incursion. Close quarters tactics only."

The two machines, heavily marked by their brawl with Mylo, moved in on the building's main entrance. Number Three's rear left leg was wobbly, causing the machine to vibrate as it walked.

"Lieutenant Belanger?" Thomas spoke into his radio.

"Yes, sir?"

"Got any Pterosaur rifles over there?"

"Got plenty in the MEAVs, Captain."

"Copy that." Thomas made eye contact with Archer and Charity. "You ready?"

Archer nodded.

Charity was a little less gung-ho. All the same, she was not going to waste any time.

"Let's go."

CHAPTER 15

Stephen Yuel had sunk into a folding chair one of the staff had brought out for his convenience. He was embarrassed to feel so exhausted, especially while watching the aftermath of the night's events. Medevacs were coming and going, getting some of the wounded out from inside the surface station and its perimeter. Many were zipped up in black bags, never to see the light of day ever again.

Through the radio feeds, he heard chatter from Raptor Pack. They had accessed a stairwell and were on their way to Sublevel-One, where Dr. Zarek did his chemistry.

All he could hear was the doctor's voice. *"We need to do more testing."*

Every time he heard those words, Yuel's memories of Mylo being in so much misery overshadowed their meaning. His career was destroyed, as his marriage would be.

The conception of Mylo Noverre was a secret he carried for many decades. Being in public service, there was a fair amount of female attention that came his way. Eventually, he broke. Things happened; lo and behold, years later he found out he had a son. Not only that, but that son was deployed to Iraq, where he had gotten the crap blown out of him by a group run by Khurto Tbileti.

That name added more weight to the burden on Yuel's shoulders. Two secrets, his illegitimate child and illegitimate affiliation, collided. Both were nearly killed on that fateful day. Fast-forward years later, both saw new glory in the form of Ecclesiastes particles. For Mylo, it was rejuvenation of his body. For Tbileti, it was power and money. Emphasis on the latter, considering his 'client' was paying top dollar for it.

In Yuel's eyes, it was just business. As long as he was blind to the casualties, he would have no trouble sleeping at night. But here he was, on the homeland, having witnessed his own son get turned into a biological weapon.

And it was all his fault.

Right and wrong do exist, no matter how one tries to complicate it with layers of relativity. Yuel was the type to do such things, especially when taking special 'gifts' from campaign contributors, or running special projects for the Military Industrial Complex.

Today, all of those veils were stripped away. Tonight, he was looking at pure, horrifying death. The difference between right and wrong was listening to General Kilmore when told the meteorite was not safe in Granger Valley, as well as heeding Dr. Zarek's warnings about the formula.

There was no relativity. No grey area. No justification.

He was simply, plainly, wrong.

All he wanted to do now was make it right.

"Copy that." General Kilmore was a few feet away, communicating with Captain Rodney of Raptor Pack. Drey Whiteford was with him, assisting with coordinates to stairwells that would lead to Sublevel-Three. Many of the elevators were out of commission, probably a direct result of Mylo attempting to slow down any assault teams. "How's the power in the lab?"

"Seems to be functioning just fine," Captain Rodney replied.

"The mutant's in the containment room," Howard Tate announced. *"He's working on the shell. You guys are gonna need to hurry it up."*

"Going as fast as we can," an annoyed Charity Black said.

"There's no way around it," Thomas said. *"I'm sending the mountain lions in. They'll be heading down Stairwell 2-B. Howard, can you take manual control?"*

"Of one of them, yeah. That'll reduce the likelihood of unintentional damage."

"See if you can lure him out of there," Thomas said. *"He's up for a good fight."*

"There's an empty containment room thirty yards southeast from where X41 is being held," Whiteford said. "There's no hazardous materials there. That'll be your best bet to slow him down."

"Copy that," Howard said. *"On it now."*

"Good luck, team." Kilmore had the look of a nervous parent as he waited for the operation to unfold. "Please Lord, let them be safe."

Yuel's eyes went to the ground. Everyone knew the odds were not in their favor. More importantly, he hated sitting here, doing nothing to stop the catastrophe he authored.

He stood up from the chair.

"Going somewhere, Senator?" Kilmore asked him.

Yuel started for the facility's main entrance. "I have an office in there. I need to check something out."

"In there?" Kilmore said. "What could be so important that you would have to go in there *now*?"

"I'll be out shortly." He spoke sternly. It was a tone that warned the general not to ask any more questions. Technically, the senator held authority over him, and Kilmore knew this. Because he wasn't stupid, Kilmore knew the senator was lying. The 'what' and 'why' Yuel was lying, he had no clue, and he wasn't going to bother asking.

Yuel entered the station, waving off one of the guards who tried to warn him of the danger. He pierced the darkness and took a right, heading *away* from the office and instead to the nearest stairwell.

***

Thomas and Archer stood by the hallway door. The two mountain lions had made their way out of the corridor to a wide stairwell, which took them to Sublevel-Two. From there, they had to follow a precise pathway to get to the tightly sealed Sublevel-Three.

Mylo knew what he was doing when he disabled the elevators. There were only two stairways that led down to that level, and both of them were narrow. Only the freight elevator was believed to be functional. Mylo, having known the codes, locked it down with a security override, essentially freezing the machine in place. And, being as savvy as he was ruthless, he was able to change the code, preventing Whiteford from accessing it remotely.

In the lab, Zarek and Charity worked tirelessly, synthesizing a never-before-used liquid serum.

"Not to cast doubt at the last minute…" the captain said, "but, how exactly are you going to target the regenerative capabilities? I mean, you said that fish played a large part in your original formula, and that was intended to maximize the immune system. How would this do the opposite?"

"Simple. We're not using the same species of fish," Zarek said.

"Beg your pardon?" Thomas said.

"I've made a lot of discoveries, Captain," Zarek explained. "Some hold the key to longer life and prosperity, but others spell disaster."

Charity walked over to a small aquarium where a disk-shaped fish swam in tight circles. Like the Gorgo fish, it was translucent, with a few colors on its spinal column and belly.

"Unlike the Gorgo fish, I'm actually familiar with this one," she explained. "It's called a Muerte Lenta. Means 'slow death'. Like the Gorgo fish, it has a lateral line full of bio-illuminating fluid. In that fluid is a bacteria that attacks stem cells and platelets. Essentially, it acts like a virus, killing the host's ability to heal itself."

"All we're doing is enhancing it with one tiny speck of the Ecclesiastes particle. In essence, we're creating our own mutation to *stop* a mutation."

Thomas knew he was getting the cliff notes version. Even so, he wasn't sure he liked what he heard. As discussed before, either this would work, or it could potentially make Mylo even stronger.

Archer had already been given the high-powered tranquilizer gun. He relinquished the Pterosaur to Thomas and awaited his special ammunition from the doctors.

"I'm through!" Howard exclaimed. *"My boys are on their way to the containment center now."*

Zarek perked up. "His boys?" He looked at Charity. "Has a real affection for his machines, doesn't he?"

She rolled her eyes. "Don't get me started."

***

The murderous beast worked on the small screws and clamps that kept the large sphere together. From the laymen, the containment sphere resembled a giant metal walnut, connected to several large mechanical branches that secured it to the center of the room. It was a large chamber in which it was held, making Mylo feel relatively small for once.

If it wasn't for the ghastly physical alterations, Mylo would have looked like any other handyman, gradually working out the weaknesses of the large sphere. A thin seam ran across the middle of the sphere where the two halves enclosed over the precious cargo inside. Unlike human maintenance crews, he did not require tools. After all, he possessed the strength to tear apart blast doors. The little imperfections of the sphere, while tiresome and requiring a little bit of concentration, were nothing but a small inconvenience.

Once X41 was free of its containment sphere, the beast would deliver it to the freight elevator. There, he would activate his new code and bring the machine topside at high speed.

Then he would give G.O.R.E. Sector and the rest of humanity a gift they would not soon forget.

First, he needed to carefully release the piece of rock without damaging it. One wrong move and he could expel its particle payload down here. Not exactly conducive to what he had in mind.

Click! Click! Click!

Mylo stopped and listened.

The sounds were metallic—literally, metal on metal, coming from one of the nearby passageways. There were subtle vibrations caused by nothing other than turning gears.

In addition, he detected a faint smell of oil and grease that was not there before. It was a combination of sounds and odors he had recently experienced.

The robots.

He stood up and stood behind the sphere. Anyone or anything that would dare open fire on him would risk shooting through the case and breaching the meteorite.

Crouching, he watched the east door, bellowing, "I hear you!"

They appeared on the other side of the entrance. Like Great Danes, they stood tall and stoic, the visors on their silver faces flashing at the former marine. There were no humans down here with them. No Raptor Pack, no Whiteford. Just the robots.

"Cowards!" the beast bellowed. "Can't fight man-to-man, so you send your toys down here to do the job for you."

The machines stood side-by-side, their turrets inactive.

From their speakers came a voice.

"You know, you look kinda like an undercooked bratwurst with that swollen head and husky shoulders."

Mylo was taken aback. He had expected many things from his enemies. But a direct insult? That was something that, even to his own surprise, was getting under his skin.

"Wait till I get ahold of you," he growled. "Once I break your droids and kill your friends, I'll show you how a bratwurst is cooked. I'll hold you over a hot fire, watch your skin blister, smell the odor coming off your meat…"

"Yeah-yeah, 'Mylo mad, Mylo smash, Mylo not have good appetite'. I get it. Can we fight now?"

Mylo remained near the sphere, not trusting the G.O.R.E. Sector person in control of the bots.

"You think I'm stupid?" he growled.

"Actually, yes."

Mylo huffed and puffed.

"Can't blame you for being too scared to come out. I mean, your balls literally did drop off. Then again, I guess they weren't much to begin with, huh?"

His temper boiled. Like vapor caught in a high wind, his plans were swept from his mind. The beast, driven by his aggression, emerged from behind the sphere and charged.

One of the robots attempted to come right at him. Mylo, watching the movements of its front legs, accurately anticipated its efforts to bludgeon him across the face.

The robot rose on its hind legs and attempted a swing.

Mylo caught the thing by its arm, pivoted on his feet, and like a Judo expert, threw the robot over his shoulder.

It came down on its back directly in front of him.

The beast raised his foot and brought it down hard on its neck, crunching the metal with a thunderous impact. The robot's motions slowed and became irregular, its computer system malfunctioning and its circuits failing.

Mylo, sensing the other one about to attack from behind, swung a backhanded strike. The bot was caught across the face and knocked against the door frame, busting a five-foot section of wall.

Returning his focus to the 'dying' robot, Mylo raised his foot as high as he could.

His heel came down.

Crash!

The machine twitched and sparked, its head pancaked, the rest of it reduced to scrap metal.

Mylo turned around and grinned at the remaining foe.

"One to go."

The machine backed into the corridor, the visor staring at him, relaying the view of Mylo's snarling face to the man controlling it.

"Too bad the mutation doesn't come with a good dentist plan."

Shrieking maniacally, the mutant sprinted.

The robot turned around and ran southeast down Corridor 3-E—straight to Containment Room Charlie.

***

"Are you guys close to being ready? Because this guy's really ticked off! He just busted another one of my mountain lions."

Even in these circumstances, Thomas could not help but grin at hearing Howard's concern for his robots.

"Are you leading him to the other containment room?"

"Heading there now. Not sure if I'll be able to keep him busy for very long."

"Okay. We're finishing up. Just keep him there as long as possible." Thomas looked over at the doctors. "You *are* almost done, right?"

"Just another minute," a sweating Dr. Zarek said.

The synthesizer beeped and chimed, mixing an unholy blend of chemicals, bio-organic material, and one single Ecclesiastes particle all together.

It went down a long, thin funnel, into a thick metal container that looked like a futuristic coffee thermos.

"We got it!" Charity exclaimed. She took the special dart from a metal case and inserted its needle through a slot in the side of the container. The base of the dart was filled with the new, untested formula, and presented to Archer. "You've got one shot. To most people, I'd say 'make it count'. But to you, I know I have nothing to worry about."

The sniper took the dart and loaded it into his rifle.

Thomas held the Pterosaur rifle at port arms. "Time to find out if this was a good or bad idea."

Charity scooped up her own rifle and gestured at the doorway. "You first."

Thomas snorted. "How polite of you."

They dashed out of the room and made a right, following the route to Stairwell 2-B.

***

Machine and mutant moved in a circle, sizing one another up. Mylo bumped his chest like a gorilla, psyching himself up for the thrill of tearing that hunk of metal apart piece by piece.

"You know, you're not smart," the man behind the speaker said.

Mylo grunted. "Says the coward."

"I might be a coward... but I'm also the one with the gun."

The turret reactivated and rose from the center of the droid's back.

Mylo shuddered, realizing he had played right into his enemy's hands by succumbing to the insults hurled at him.

A spray of ammunition punched through his meat, doubling him over. More shots struck his chest and shoulders, rolling him onto his back.

The mutation roared, his nerves flooding his body with obnoxious pain signals. It was a short-lived hazard, for the gift given to him by Dr. Zarek was quick to start patching him up. Pieces of lead were pushed from his body onto the tile floor, the holes quickly closing with new flesh.

A third blast tore into Mylo, angering him further.

Roaring, he got back to his feet and sprinted through the line of bullets, absorbing each one as he closed in on the robot.

Bam!

He put his shoulder into the impact, knocking his opponent backward. The robot spun a hundred-eighty degrees, its gun facing away from its target.

Mylo reached over and grabbed the turret. Pulling up, he removed the droid's primary weapon with brute force.

Holding the broken gun by its muzzle, he struck the robot on the back of its head, as though punishing an unruly dog with a newspaper.

The robot retaliated with a heavy mull kick from one of its back legs, driving the mutant back. It rotated left and swung one of its arms, connecting with Mylo's elbow with enough force to break the spine protruding from the joint.

The beast shrieked, feeling literal bone detaching from his body.

Another swing from the clubbed mechanical feet caught him on the jaw, separating a couple of teeth. It was followed up by a high-pitched blast of sound that burst the overhead lights and any glass that was nearby.

Mylo staggered on wobbly legs, his eardrums literally blown out.

A clubbing hit to the chest put him on his back.

"Ooooo! That looked like it hurt."

The words were close, yet sounded as though they were miles away. The dog-shaped machine circled the mutant, positioning itself for another strike.

Each step was heard more clearly, for the creature's rapid recovery fixed all of his senses. The broken spines on his elbow took new form, new teeth grew from his gums, and a bad temper fueled his strength.

The robot moved in for the kill, raising its front legs to bash his skull in.

Mylo rolled in a reverse summersault, evading the attack. The droid struck the floor, caving it in twelve inches deep. Its head shifted, pointing its visor at the now-standing mutant, almost in shock that he had moved so fast.

A booming howl filled the room. Mylo threw himself at the droid, grabbing it by the hind quarters and lifting it off the floor like a wrestler.

The robot was slammed to the ground, jamming the gears for its right shoulder joint.

He picked it up again, now raising it high over his head. For the second time, it was thrown hard against the floor.

Lost in madness, the man-beast began hammering his fists on the robot, gradually deforming it. Parts came loose. Smoke burst from the joints and CPU. Sparks zipped from the crunching heap like miniature shooting stars.

In the end, it was a pile of unrecognizable scrap.

Mylo stood tall over his foe, taking satisfaction in its new, useless condition. If there was any disappointment in this victory, it came from the fact that he did not take a real life.

Then again, there was plenty of that coming in the near future. The *very* near future—in less than five minutes, he would have the ultimate weapon at his disposal.

He departed the chamber and hurried down the corridor to retrieve X41.

***

They were almost there. Zarek's codes to access the third floor worked, and the trio of monster hunters quickly descended into the bottom level of the Granger Valley Research Facility.

It was almost alien in its design, the overhead a jet black color with long LED tubes running down the entire length like veins. Each tunnel seemed to stretch forever, and every inch was carefully designed with the latest technology.

The lights had dimmed to a greenish color.

Down Corridor 2-E, they were completely dark for a section of twenty feet, save for a few sparks spitting from a ruptured point in the wall. Giant footsteps echoed from the north, gradually growing farther away.

"Talk to me, Howard," Thomas said through the radio.

"All mountain lions are out of commission," the engineer said in a bitter voice. *"Target's heading back to the meteorite. I tried to keep him busy as long as I could. Guys, he's almost got that thing free."*

"Copy that." Thomas doubled his pace and signaled to his teammates to do the same. "Let's move!"

***

The beast turned the corner, stepping over the worthless wreckage that was the second droid. It was a sight that signified what was wrong with modern warfare. Military leaders relied too much on technology. Drone strikes, satellites, computers running submarines. Back in the day, it was man against man, with nothing but swords and axes.

In a few minutes, Mylo would have his army. Sure, the mutants would have no true allegiance to him, but they would do his work all the same. The country that had ruined his human body and subjected him to a decade of unbearable pain would have its punishment. The mutants would spread across the countryside and invade every town. In twenty-four hours, human casualties would skyrocket into the tens of thousands. G.O.R.E. Sector would be in over its head figuring out how to contain the situation.

He went to the sphere and resumed freeing the meteorite. The last of the bolts were no match for his rugged strength.

Lifting the top of the sphere like an oyster shell, he laid eyes on the large chunk of rock.

It was beige in color, darkened near some pores where the drills had extracted some of the mineral. Its texture was bumpy, similar to a crab's shell. Even with a gentle touch, he could sense how hollow it was.

This was more than a simple rock hurtling through space. The universe had a beef with the inhabitants of Earth and had delivered this ultimate weapon to punish them.

"If it is the universe's will... then I shall be the enforcer!"

"No!"

Mylo jerked his head to the side.

It was a familiar voice; one that was simultaneously comforting and incensing.

He turned to look at the room's west doors.

Standing there, unarmed and alone, was his father.

For most of his life, Mylo only knew him as Senator Yuel. It wasn't until his mother reached out to him that the senator learned the truth. Never once did he refer to him as 'Dad'. There was no point. Yuel was just a grubbing career politician, with little regard for anything that did not advance his position. As far as helping Mylo with getting his job and getting treatment, it was fair to assume he did it to prevent his mother from going to the press with the truth of their affair.

Yet, none of this explained why the man was here alone.

"You!" the beast roared.

"It's me," Yuel said in a calm, shaky voice. With his hands raised, he stepped into the chamber. His eyes were moist, his hair a mess of grit and sweat, his fancy suit unbuttoned. "Mylo, I'm sorry."

The beast huffed. His desire to kill was welling up. The fact that he recognized this man as his biological father did not prevent that. If anything, it riled him up even more.

He stomped in Yuel's direction, shoulders high, teeth bared.

"Fool!"

Yuel stood firm. There were a few twitches in his leg as the natural drive to flee blared alarms in his mind. He was breathing through his mouth now, trying to form words in the midst of utter fright.

"Yes. I am a fool. I did this to you. Everything wrong with your life, it was my fault."

Mylo exhaled. A sense of intrigue delayed the smashing of his fist against the senator's head. He had never heard the man speak this way before. He certainly was not the type to put himself in danger, yet here he was, standing before Mylo Noverre.

"I've done you wrong, Mylo. More than you know," he continued. "There's so many sins I have to answer for. Not being there for you is one of them. But the worst is doing...THIS, to you." He moved his hands in an uncoordinated circle, gesturing at Mylo's form. "Had I known you were in the world, I would have done things differently."

The beast exhaled, wetting his face with moisture.

Yuel stood his ground. If there was anything he could do right in his life, it was not to fail his son this one last time.

"You're not a murderer, Mylo. You are a good man. You just got turned into something else. That is my fault. I'm sorry." Slowly, he put his hand out. Mylo stood still, letting the man's palm touch his grey, bumpy wrist.

Father and son stood quietly for a moment, the latter watching the tiny hand move over his own.

"Stop the violence," Yuel said. He looked his son in the eyes. "No more violence."

Mylo returned the gaze. There was an odd feeling of gentleness in the way he was breathing now. A sense of calm breezed into the room.

Yuel quivered, hoping his appeal to the humanity of the man inside the monster was successful.

His hands began to jitter after watching those eyes slant and that ugly tongue rolling over those carnivorous teeth.

A demonic laugh burst from the back of Mylo's throat.

"No!"

He raised his hand and struck his father.

Senator Yuel flew across the room and struck the wall.

Mylo stomped over to him, taking joy in the blood pooling from the man's mouth. Many bones had been shattered and the internal damage was beyond severe. He was still alive, gasping for breath.

"Now, you know pain!" the beast growled.

He lifted his foot to squish Yuel like an ant.

BANG!

Mylo stumbled forward, grunting as a high-caliber bullet pierced his back. Stepping over his father, he regained his balance.

Before he could turn around, another burst of pain made him recoil. This one was smaller, lacking the crack of a gunshot. On the contrary, it felt similar to a needle prick.

In the following moments, Mylo came to realize that mental image was probably more precise than he thought. His stomach churned, his head throbbed, and his insides felt as though they were in a storm.

He reached behind his back and pulled the dart out of his flesh.

Sure enough, they had injected him with something.

He turned around and laid eyes on the three G.O.R.E. Sector specialists. They stood at the doorway, all carrying high-caliber sniper rifles of a design he had never seen before.

He remembered their names from when they met during his final day as a human. Thomas Rodney, Dr. Charity Black, and Ray Archer.

Lying at their feet was a Remington 937, engineered specifically for Granger to be used for sedating unruly test subjects.

The beast growled. Had it not been for his father's distraction, he would have heard and smelled them coming long ago. Not that it mattered; these three would be no match for him, even with those fancy guns.

He held the dart in front of his eyes.

Poison?

He taunted them with a gravelly laugh.

"You'll need more than that to kill me."

"That's correct, Corporal Noverre," Thomas said.

He fired a shot.

Mylo jolted. The bullet entered his chest and cut into his lungs. He leaned forward slightly, feeling the air rushing out of him as though he was a deflating balloon. It was a feeling he was accustomed to. Getting shot was becoming nothing more than a minor setback. Sure, it presented a fair amount of pain, but there was also a rush of endorphins he felt, which signaled that the body was getting right to work fixing him up.

Oddly enough, he was not feeling that rush now. As a matter of fact, his back was still throbbing from where he was shot before the injection.

He touched his finger to the small of his back, feeling the wound and the blood pouring out of it.

His eyes went to the members of Raptor Pack.

They had managed to incapacitate his regenerative capabilities.

Snarling like a wild animal, he attempted to rush them.

BANG! BANG! BANG! BANG!

Numerous shots struck his chest and throat.

Mylo dropped to one knee, his vision fading. All the strength in the world made no difference now, not with his airway and heart turned to Swiss cheese. He tried to stand up. He had the perfect plan. G.O.R.E. Sector would be no match for his army of mutants. He was so close.

In the end, he failed.

The life left his eyes and the beast fell forward.

Thomas reloaded his Pterosaur and took in a sigh of relief. "Nice work, Charity."

"Thanks, Cap," she replied, equally calmed by the positive result of her work.

After confirming that the beast was, in fact, deceased, they rushed to the injured senator.

"General Kilmore, the target is neutralized. Mission success. We need a medical team down here on the double. Senator Yuel is severely injured."

"Damn it. Copy that. Well done, Raptor Pack."

"Oh, geez, Mr. Yuel," Charity said. "What the hell are you doing down here?" The politician winced, his mouth bloody. He raised a hand and put it on her shoulder. Comfortingly, she touched his wrist. "No, no. You don't actually need to answer that. Just hold on. We'll get you to a hospital."

He shook his head. "N-no... There's... something... you must know." He paused to make sure all three of them were listening. The tremors intensified, as though death was forcibly trying to tear his soul from his body.

"What is it, Senator?" Thomas asked.

Yuel bobbed his head, fighting for every second of life he could spare.

"I—Iraq. There's a black site... Near a village— Taza. We found another meteor. It's held... in... a... b- bunker. Moran's there. And Khurto Tbileti... they're working together…" He coughed and gagged. His fingers coiled into claws and his arms bent at the elbows. "It's… my fault…"

The fight was over.

After a failed effort to resuscitate him, Charity closed the man's eyes.

Thomas stood up to speak into the radio. "General?"

"Go ahead."

"The senator is deceased. We're heading topside."

CHAPTER 16

"You're kidding," Renee exclaimed.

Thomas shook his head. The team stood outside *Firebird-Two*, keeping a fair distance away from the facility personnel as they ran their recovery sweep of the facility. It was not a job Thomas envied, for they would be hauling bodies and injured people out of there all night. Unfortunately, given the ferocity of the mutant's rampage, it was likely to be more of the former than the latter.

"I wish I was."

"There's another meteor?" Howard said. "And the senator was working with somebody to excavate it?"

"Did he happen to mention *who*?" Renee asked.

"If you're referring to Brom-Caylen, no," Charity said.

"But he did mention Moran by name," Thomas said. "Plus another— Khurto Tbileti. I'm familiar with that name, unfortunately. He's a warlord. Calls himself a freedom fighter, but don't kid yourselves. He's after power. Odds are, Senator Yuel was funding his operation in exchange for locating the meteorite."

Howard crossed his arms. "So, if we're going to go after the rock, we're gonna have to go through that guy."

"I can't imagine the government authorizing a strike against a foreign land," Kilmore said.

"There are local rebels in that region," Thomas said. "They've been trying to liberate the villages from insurgent control for years. I say, we point them in the right direction. And provide a little support, off the books. Besides, it'll give us a chance to give that Moran fellow a nice hello."

Renee cracked her knuckles. "I do owe him for what he did to my last ride." She went up the ramp. "What are we waiting for? Let's go."

"First thing's first," Thomas said. He entered the MEAV and went to the cooler. "I need a beer. Or eight, or ten."

Kilmore managed to laugh at that one.

"Don't we all?"

Check out other great
Cryptid Novels!

J.H. Moncrieff

RETURN TO DYATLOV PASS

In 1959, nine Russian students set off on a skiing expedition in the Ural Mountains. Their mutilated bodies were discovered weeks later. Their bizarre and unexplained deaths are one of the most enduring true mysteries of our time. Nearly sixty years later, podcast host Nat McPherson ventures into the same mountains with her team, determined to finally solve the mystery of the Dyatlov Pass incident. Her plans are thwarted on the first night, when two trackers from her group are brutally slaughtered. The team's guide, a superstitious man from a neighboring village, blames the killings on yetis, but no one believes him. As members of Nat's team die one by one, she must figure out if there's a murderer in their midst—or something even worse—before history repeats itself and her group becomes another casualty of the infamous Dead Mountain.

Gerry Griffiths

CRYPTID ZOO

As a child, rare and unusual animals, especially cryptid creatures, always fascinated Carter Wilde. Now that he's an eccentric billionaire and runs the largest conglomerate of high-tech companies all over the world, he can finally achieve his wildest dream of building the most incredible theme park ever conceived on the planet... CRYPTID ZOO. Even though there have been apparent problems with the project, Wilde still decides to send some of his marketing employees and their families on a forced vacation to assess the theme park in preparation for Opening Day. Nick Wells and his family are some of those chosen and are about to embark on what will become the most terror-filled weekend of their lives—praying they survive. STEP RIGHT UP AND GET YOUR FREE PASS... TO CRYPTID ZOO

Check out other great
Cryptid Novels!

P.K. Hawkins

THE CRYPTID FILES

Fresh out of the academy with top marks, Agent Bradley Tennyson is expecting to have the pick of cases and investigations throughout the country. So he's shocked when instead he is assigned as the new partner to "The Crag," an agent well past his prime. He thinks the assignment is a punishment. It's anything but. Agent George Crag has been doing this job for far longer than most, and he knows what skeletons his bosses have in the closet and where the bodies are buried. He has pretty much free reign to pick his cases, and he knows exactly which one he wants to use to break in his new young partner: the disappearance and murder of a couple of college kids in a remote mountain town. Tennyson doesn't realize it, but Crag is about to introduce him to a world he never believed existed: The Cryptid Files, a world of strange monsters roaming in the night. Because these murders have been going on for a long time, and evidence is mounting that the murderer may just in fact be the legendary Bigfoot.

Gerry Griffiths

DOWN FROM BEAST MOUNTAIN

A beast with a grudge has come down from the mountain to terrorize the townsfolk of Porterville. The once sleepy town is suddenly wide awake. Sheriff Abel McGuire and game warden Grant Tanner frantically investigate one brutal slaying after another as they follow the blood trail they hope will eventually lead to the monstrous killer. But they better hurry and stop the carnage before the census taker has to come out and change the population sign on the edge of town to ZERO.

Check out other great

Cryptid Novels!

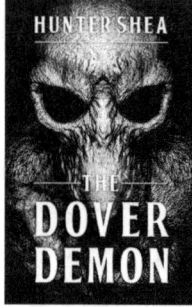

Hunter Shea

THE DOVER DEMON

The Dover Demon is real...and it has returned. In 1977, Sam Brogna and his friends came upon a terrifying, alien creature on a deserted country road. What they witnessed was so bizarre, so chilling, they swore their silence. But their lives were changed forever. Decades later, the town of Dover has been hit by a massive blizzard. Sam's son, Nicky, is drawn to search for the infamous cryptid, only to disappear into the bowels of a secret underground lair. The Dover Demon is far deadlier than anyone could have believed. And there are many of them. Can Sam and his reunited friends rescue Nicky and battle a race of creatures so powerful, so sinister, that history itself has been shaped by their secretive presence? "THE DOVER DEMON is Shea's most delightful and insidiously terrifying monster yet." – Shotgun Logic Reviews "An excellent horror novel and a strong standout in the UFO and cryptid subgenres." –Hellnotes "Non-stop action awaits those brave enough to dive into the small town of Dover, and if you're lucky, you won't see the Demon himself!" – The Scary Reviews PRAISE FOR SWAMP MONSTER MASSACRE "B-horror movie fans rejoice, Hunter Shea is here to bring you the ultimate tale of terror!" – Horror Novel Reviews "A nonstop thrill ride! I couldn't put this book down." – Cedar Hollow Horror Reviews

Armand Rosamilia

THE BEAST

The end of summer, 1986. With only a few days left until the new school year, twins Jeremy and Jack Schaffer are on very different paths. Jeremy is the geek, playing Dungeons & Dragons with friends Kathleen and Randy, while Jack is the jock, getting into trouble with his buddies. And then everything changes when neighbor Mister Higgins is killed by a wild animal in his yard. Was it a bear? There's something big lurking in the woods behind their New Jersey home. Will the police be able to solve the murder before more Middletown residents are ripped apart?